THE DAY OF THE PEPPERCORN KILL

THE DAY OF THE PEPPERCORN KILL

John Wainwright

St. Martin's Press
New York

First printed in Great Britain.
Copyright © 1981 by John Wainwright
For information, write: St. Martin's Press,
175 Fifth Avenue, New York, N.Y. 10010
Manufactured in the United States of America

Library of Congress Cataloging in Publication Data

Wainwright, John William, 1921-
    The day of the peppercorn kill.

    I. Title.
PR6073.A354D3   1981   823'.914   81-8722
ISBN 0-312-18420-4   AACR2

To bring the dead to life
Is no great magic.
Few are wholly dead;
Blow on a dead man's embers
And a live flame will start.

To Bring the Dead to Life
Robert Graves

THE DAY OF THE
PEPPERCORN KILL

SATURDAY, JULY 14th...

The door chimes rang once. Just the once; as if whoever had pressed the bell-push had merely touched it, then removed his finger.

His finger.

The woman didn't have any doubt. She said, 'Damn!', but the small swear word was directed more at the inconvenience of the chimes than at their unexpectedness. At *his* inconsiderate timing.

She'd been waiting for the four-note summons of the chimes for more than twelve hours. For almost twenty-four hours. Waiting? We-ell—no . . . not exactly *waiting*. Anticipating. That was nearer the mark. Anticipating his arrival; contemplating how she'd face up to it; what she'd say; what *he'd* say.

Last night, for example, she'd pleaded a headache. She'd cancelled the dinner-date and insisted upon an evening alone. And she'd sat there, expecting the bastard. True, she hadn't gone in for the candlelight, slinky-dress ploy. That would have been . . . *obscene*. That would have been too much; a cheapening of herself and, in a way, an insult to him. It might have embarrassed him. It *would* have embarrassed him . . . it would have embarrassed both of them.

Nevertheless . . .

The meal had been prepared, and waiting; the lobster salad, and the wine. And, for three hours, the stereo had played Sinatra at just the right volume; not loud enough to interfere with normal conversation, but sufficiently loud to plaster over any awkward cracks in the small-talk.

The small-talk.

7

In God's name, *what* small-talk. Not coffee-morning stuff. Not cocktail party stuff. What conversation they might have had wouldn't have been 'small'. It would have been . . .

Damn it, what *would* it have been?

She was trembling; a tiny quiver which seemed to originate from every nerve-end in her whole body. A peculiar ache was building up in her jaw muscles, and she realised that she was clenching her teeth . . . hard. Her fingers had closed into fists, and the nails were biting into the palms of her hands.

She said, 'Damn!' again, and forced herself to relax, before she walked to the door.

He looked the same . . . but, oh so different.

Pale. She'd expected him to look pale; the pallor went with the . . . She'd expected him to look pale, but not so completely devoid of *colour*. Not so white. Not so wan.

And grey; his hair was grey. Not the pepper-and-salt mix she'd sometimes visualised; not the grey wings, which might have given him the standard politician's middle-aged dignity. None of these things but, instead, grey and lifeless . . . but, above all else, overall grey.

Thin? No, he didn't look thin; he'd always kept himself fit; he'd never carried surplus fat. But, somehow, *smaller*. There was a stoop to the shoulders, and the head was held down as if in perpetual shame. But, there was more than that . . . something more. As if he'd shrunk a little; as if he was made of inferior quality material and, with the washings of the last twelve years, he'd *shrunk*.

He raised his head and looked at her, and the eyes held no pride. None of the old pride, which had bordered upon arrogance. Hangdog fear, and pleading. That was the only expression they held. Other than that, they were dead eyes.

His lips moved. It might have been a smile—it was *meant* to be a smile—but it reminded her of the flicker of a cur's tail as it approached a cruel master; a desire for friendship coupled

8

with the certain knowledge of hurt.

He moistened his lips, and said, 'Is it . . .'

Instead of completing the question, he glanced beyond her, towards the hall and the inside of the house, and moved his head in a single nod.

'Oh—er—yes . . . of course.'

She opened the door wide, stood aside and moved one arm in a gesture of welcome.

'Thanks.'

Once more the whipped-cur smile touched his lips, and he walked past her and into the house.

She closed the door and followed him and, again, the trembling threatened to take over. She wasn't afraid; she hadn't been afraid of him before, and she certainly wasn't afraid of him *now*. But . . . something. Something, not too far removed from stage-fright; a tightening of the stomach muscles; a dryness of the mouth; a feeling of panic.

And, last night she'd had Sinatra waiting for him. Sinatra, lobster salad and wine . . . my God! How wrong was it possible to get? How stupid? How unintentionally cruel?

She said, 'I'll—I'll phone the office.'

'W-what?'

'Tell them I won't be in this morning.'

'Look—there's no need to . . . I mean . . .'

'It's one of the perks of being the boss.'

'Oh!'

'Find a comfortable chair. Settle in. I'll be with you.'

'Th-thanks.' He bobbed his head in a ridiculously servile nod.

'Please,' she said, softly. 'You're home. It all belongs to you.'

(*The uniformed policeman behind the counter looked very determined. Polite, but adamant.*

He said, 'I'm sorry, sir. If you'll just give me some inkling

9

of what it's about.'

'It's important.'

'That's not enough, sir. That's too vague.'

The night-shift officers made their way past him; behind him and out into the early darkness. They buttoned their macs against the midsummer rain as they neared the main entrance of the police station.

The P.C. said, 'Understand me, sir. I'm not being awkward.'

'Nor am I.'

'But, senior detectives . . . they like to know.'

'I appreciate that . . .'

'In that case, if you'll . . .'

'No!'

'Sir?'

'It's not that I don't trust you. It's not that I . . .'

The P.C. allowed the silence to stretch itself out into ten, or fifteen seconds.

Then, he said, 'A hint's all I need.'

'No.'

'Just to make sure they know it's not a wild-goose chase.'

'I'm sorry.'

'For heaven's sake, why not?' The patience of the P.C. was wearing thin.

'I'd—I'd . . . I can't tell the story twice. That's why not. Once . . . I couldn't bring myself to tell it twice.')

9 a.m. . . .

She watched him from the deep comfort of one of the twin, swivel wing rockers which flanked the sheepskin hearthrug. To her, this was the normality of good living. But, to him . . . A sense of shame hit her as she realised that the very comfort added to his discomfiture. He was awkward; he sat on the edge of the chair, with his elbows tucked into his side and clear of the arms. Tilting the chair forward; countering its ready luxury and turning pleasurableness into discomposure.

God . . . and last night, she'd had wine, and lobster salad, and Sinatra waiting!

She said, 'I'd have visited you, had you wanted me to visit.'

He seemed not to hear her.

'Y-you've made the place nice. Y'know . . . nice.' He moved his head, and the dulled eyes travelled slowly from one expensive—almost extravagant—piece to the next. The tiny Murillo of an urchin, positioned tastefully above and to one side of the mock ingle-nook. The five-bar, wrought-iron electric fire shaped as a fire-basket. The velvet drapes, tassled and drawn back from the double-glazed picture-window. The tiny, exquisite alabaster figurine of the discus thrower standing in one corner of the room on its own slender, antique plant-pot table. The eyes did a slow and deliberate tour of the room, and he muttered, 'N-nice.'

'Had you asked me to visit you, I'd have come,' she insisted.

'Y-you'll—you'll have friends.'

'What?'

'P-people who know about these things.'

'What things?'

'D-decorating. Making a house beautiful.'

'I have a friend.' Despite a deliberate effort, her voice tightened. It became fractionally brittle; fractionally harder.

He nodded, slowly.

'She's an interior decorator.' She put slight emphasis on the first word. 'She helps me, sometimes.'

Again, he nodded.

'Taste,' she said, 'isn't a gift of the Gods. Some people think it is. It isn't. Like every other talent, it has to be disciplined. Learned. Otherwise, it runs riot and dissipates itself. The end result can be ugly . . . like eating too much fresh cream can

11

make you ill. You need guidance from an expert. Unless you are an expert . . . and I'm not. She likes to help me, and I give her a free hand. I'm appreciative.'

'A f-free hand?' A keen ear might have caught a hint of sarcasm.

'I pay her. I can afford to pay her.'

'Of c-course.'

For the third time, she said, 'Had you asked me, I would have visited you.'

'Oh!'

'You didn't ask. In your letters . . . you never asked.'

'N-no.'

He held the beaker in his two closed hands, and stared at the surface of the tea.

Tea, in beakers. Not Sinatra and lobster salad. Tea, in beakers, seemed more appropriate. The nerve-ends between her shoulder blades tingled and a sudden shiver touched her skin. It was like talking to a corpse—a dead man . . . then, as the thought flickered through her mind, she felt ashamed. He'd been buried. For twelve years, he'd been entombed . . . what *else*, but a dead man?

'Was it . . . bad?' she asked, softly.

'It was a l-long way,' he muttered.

'I beg your pardon?'

'For you to c-come. It was a l-long way.'

'Darling.' She forced herself to say the word. She didn't mean it—or, did she? . . . either way, it didn't matter. Some form of endearment was necessary. Vital. Like a drowning man; whoever he was, you threw him a line, if possible. Whoever he was. Whatever he'd done.

He moistened his lips, stared at the tea for another moment, then raised his eyes to look at her face.

'Welcome home.' She worked hard to make the smile genuine.

12

'Sh-she was . . .' He fought to master the stammer, swallowed, then said, 'Sh-she wasn't what she m-made herself out to be.'

'I don't think we should . . .'

'W-w-we *should*!' It wasn't anger; he seemed incapable of any emotion as alive as anger. But there was insistence there, in that last word. As if this was a hurdle he had to surmount, before he could make progress.

She nodded, and said, 'If that's what you want.'

He moistened his lips with the near-cold tea, before he spoke. Then, he took it word at a time; as is he'd practised the speech over and over again . . . but carefully, in order not to miss a word or insert a pause which might be misconstrued.

'Sh-she wasn't a virgin. Sh-she wasn't the innocent the newspapers made her out to be. N-not what the p-police made her out to be. She was a t-tease. A whore. She'd b-been with men before. Sh-she boasted about it. In the car. Sh-she said men found her v-very s-satisfying. Her own words. It was her idea. I—I hadn't . . . W-when I first offered her a lift. Sh-she . . .'

'You picked her up.'

'Sh-she made it ab-ab-abundantly clear that . . .'

'She was only sixteen. Barely sixteen.'

'Sh-she looked older. M-much older.'

'Really?' The woman fought to keep the contempt from her tone.

The man muttered, 'I th-thought she was at l-least twenty. At least t-twenty.'

The woman pushed herself from the chair. She walked across the room; across the polished, rug-strewn floor; slowly and a little stiff-legged. She paused at a near-antique side-table, took a cigarette from a carved ebony box and lighted it from the flame of a worked-jet table-lighter. Then, she continued her stroll—still stiff-legged—until she reached the plant-pot table. As she talked she ran the tip of a forefinger along the smooth surface of the alabaster arm; from the lowered shoulder, past the twisted elbow, to the tiny hand holding the miniature discus, then back to the shoulder again. Backwards and forwards. Slowly. Deliberately. Carefully. As if using the fragility of the figurine as a bond via which to control any possible upsurge of anger. She stood with her back to him, and spoke in a quiet, controlled voice.

She said, 'Rape.'

The man remained silent.

'The rape of a sixteen-year-old schoolgirl . . . a grammar-school girl.'

The man still remained silent.

'You pleaded guilty,' she mused. 'No extenuating circumstances. You'd picked her up on the motorway. Less than five miles from home, you'd pulled into a lay-by and sexually assaulted her . . . against her will.'

'N-not against her will,' he whispered.

'You say that, now.'

'I've n-no cause to lie. N-not now.'

'Why?' she asked, sadly.

'B-because I've paid my debt to . . .'

'No! Not that. Why? Why do it? Why commit rape? Wasn't our marriage . . . complete enough? Didn't I satisfy you? Was there something missing? Did I ever refuse you? Anything? Did I ever let you down? I wasn't cold . . . I don't think I was cold. I don't think I was unresponsive. I wasn't frigid. I was a good wife . . . I tried to be a good wife. Physically. Emotionally. What we did—everything we did—was good.'

'G-good,' he breathed, and it was like the faint echo of her last word.

'Then, in God's name, *why?*'

The man thought . . .

14

Because sex, like talent, isn't a gift from the Gods. Like talent, it has to be disciplined. Monogamy is not a natural state. It has to be practised, and re-practised, every day of a man's life. With some men, practice leads to perfection. They come to accept it as natural . . . even though it isn't natural. With other men, it isn't easy. With some men, it's impossible.

With me, it wasn't easy. Sexually, you were always desirable . . . whilever you were there. You enjoyed sex. You gave as much as you received. In that, you were a perfect wife . . . but you weren't always there. And, when you weren't there, the discipline had to be very strict.

So many times, I was tempted. And, so many times I resisted temptation. I was even proud of my ability to resist temptation . . . knowing that you'd be waiting. Knowing that anything any other woman could offer you, too, could offer. Would willingly offer. Openly and without need of persuasion. Without need for secrecy.

You were a good wife. None better.

But, she was . . . different.

She smelled of sex. It was an invisible cloak she carried around with her. When she looked at you, you knew. The promise was there, in her eyes. The promise of something superb. The promise of something so magnificent as to be different.

And the talk . . . the deliberate double entendre every few sentences.

She was young, but she wasn't beautiful. She was attractive. But not beautiful. Unless sin itself is beautiful . . . in which case she was the most beautiful creature on earth.

I've dreamed of her these last twelve years. Often. I've dreamed of you, too. Of course I've dreamed of you. Thought of you. Visualised you. But not like her . . . not as much as I've dreamed and thought of her. . . .

15

The woman dragged hard on her cigarette. As she exhaled the smoke, her forefinger continued its tracing of the surface of the figurine.

She said, 'We shouldn't talk about it.'

'N-no.'

'It's past. Water under the bridge. We're only hurting ourselves by talking about it. We shouldn't *talk* about it.'

'Y-you asked,' he murmured.

'I know. I'm sorry.' She turned, walked back to her chair and, as she sat down, she said, 'I—er—I expected you yesterday. Last night. I thought you'd arrive last night.'

'F-Friday the thirteenth.' The corners of his lips lifted fractionally.

'What? Oh!' Her ghost-smile met his ghost-smile. 'Don't tell me you've grown superstitious.'

'C-careful. I don't take ch-chances.'

'Where did you spend the night?'

'The S-Salvation Army. They put on a v-very good breakfast.'

'Good. I'm pleased.'

'Eggs and b-bacon and f-fried tom-tom-tom . . .' The word defeated him and, for a moment, he looked as if he might break down.

'Don't!' she said, softly.

'I'm s-sorry.' It was a little like a breathed groan of despair.

'Don't be.'

'I d-didn't used to be . . . B-before I went to p-prison, I could . . .'

'Darling, *I* know what you were like.'

He closed his eyes, lowered his head and nodded, slowly.

She thought she had never before seen a human being so drained of life. Of vitality. Of the will to live. She leaned forward and, in her free hand, took the beaker of cold tea from his fingers.

16

She said, 'There's plenty of hot water. Soap. Salts. Clean towels. Why don't you take a bath, darling? You'll feel better. Then . . . lobster salad? Let's go a little crazy. Lobster salad, with wine, and Sinatra singing in the background. Never mind that it's still morning. You're home, darling. Let's celebrate.'

9.10 a.m. . . .

Ralph Finney bawled, 'For Christ's sake! Turn that bloody transistor down. You wearing earplugs, or something?'

The shouted protest didn't even scratch the barrier of sound coming from the kitchen.

Finney blew out his cheeks in disgust and concentrated his attention upon his breakfast kippers.

Kippers, for Christ's sake! What the hell good were kippers to a man who grafted his heart out anything up to fourteen hours a day? Supermarket kippers. Ready-wrapped in cellophane, complete with butter-pat. Boned. Coloured. Damn near tasteless. The stupid bitch couldn't even buy *real* kippers. And, if she did, she couldn't fry the bloody things. Instant coffee . . . because the workings of a percolator were well beyond her bird-brain capacity. Ready-sliced bread . . . because if she ever handled a bread-knife she'd cut her damn-fool fingers off. Even the toast was burned. Even the butter was so much yellow slop, because she hadn't put it in the fridge overnight.

Holy cow, she got worse by the year . . . worse by the bloody day.

He slopped coffee past his lips, to empty his mouth, filled his lungs and yelled, 'You hear me? *Turn that sodding volume down.*'

'Wassat?'

Myra Finney appeared at the door leading to the kitchen. Her stained house-coat fell about six inches short of her nightdress, and the hem of her nightdress was torn, leaving a loop of cheap lace which threatened to catch in the toe of her worn-out mules.

She pushed a strand of hair from the front of her eyes with the back of her hand, and said, 'You say something?'

'Don't tell me you *heard* me?' Finney's sarcasm was as heavy as his thick-limbed body.

'Eh?'

'That pop crap you have on in there.'

'I like it.'

'It's crap.'

'There's no accounting for taste.'

'Taste? What the hell do *you* know about taste?'

'I sometimes wonder . . . I married *you*.'

'Turn the bloody thing down,' snapped Finney.

'I'm listening to it.'

'Okay—listen . . . but don't make the whole damn street listen.'

'I like it loud.'

'Hey.' Finney waved a fork gently, but threateningly, at her. 'I'm not asking favours. I'm not even saying "please". Turn that bleeding thing down—right now . . . or I come in there and put my heel through it, and stop it forever. Okay?'

'You would, too.' Her nostrils quivered with suppressed anger.

'You bet. I bought it . . . I'll kill it. No arguments. Turn it down . . . *well* down.'

She turned and returned to the kitchen. The volume decreased drastically, and Finney's mouth moved into a satisfied grin.

Like ready-made kippers. Ready-made background noise . . . and, like crappy kippers, crappy noise. Everything too much of everything. Her, too. Too much bloody lipstick, too much bloody eye-shadow . . . when she got round to it. Too much tit and too much arse. She'd lost her figure, way back

18

when. Not bad—not *too* bad . . . just too much of everything, and not enough of some things. Not enough class. Not enough *soap*, sometimes. Since the kids had come along, she'd grown sloppy. Just that shade more sloppy, every time. Three kids. What were three kids, for Christ's sake? Some dames dropped twice that number, and still kept themselves smart. Still kept themselves neat and bedworthy.

But, this one . . .

Judas Priest! Sometimes she reminded him of a sow, between the sheets.

And she couldn't even cook. A can-opener and a transistor were the two most important things in her whole damn life.

But easy, boy—easy . . . don't get too steamed up.

How long since, now?

A year? No . . . more than a year. Nearly eighteen months. And, he'd gone over the top *that* night. He'd smacked her around, and given her what she'd been begging for for years. Very nice, very satisfying, but very noisy. That had been *some* night. Her screaming, him belting her and swearing fit to bust, and the kids yelling. It had been needed. It had been long overdue. And, it had done good. She didn't argue much, since. Not as much yap. Sulks, maybe . . . but she knew when to keep her cake-hole zipped.

Except that some damn-fool neighbour had dialled nine-nine-nine.

Nine-nine-nine, for Christ's sake!

Red necks all round . . . except for Gilliant. Gilliant had threatened to slice him down two rungs. *And,* he'd meant it. Because Gilliant was a 'book boy'. Yackety-yackety, act and section—yackety-yackety, rules and regulations . . . and, 'Police officers are expected to set a standard of behaviour, Finney.'

Up a duck's tail-end.

Police officers (Chief Constable, Mister-bloody-Gilliant, sir)

19

are expected to stamp out the germs of humanity. They don't do that . . . they're no damn good. Police officers have one job. To make damn sure the screws inside H.M. Prisons are *not* under-employed. Because (with respect, Chief Constable, Mister-bloody-Gilliant, sir) all your fancy acts and sections—all your crap-arsed rules and regulations—were written and compiled by stupid gits who, like yourself, 'expect police officers to set a standard of behaviour'. Except the bastards don't have standards, and we poor buggers who have to climb into the swill-bin to get our hands on 'em—we poor buggers who don't sit around in posh, air-conditioned offices—we *know* things. We know things you'll *never* know. That 'please' and 'thank you' isn't the way to do it. Ever! Which makes us rough—rough as the wrong end of a pineapple . . . and we stand so much from anybody. Anybody! And that (Mister Chief Constable Gilliant) is *why*.

I knocked the cow around, because she *deserved* to be knocked around.

Like now—with these crummy kippers and this lousy coffee . . . she *deserves* a belt across the chops. That's all she has to do. Feed me. That's all I ask . . . a full belly and a bit o' peace and quiet.

And—Jesus wept!—she can't even give me *that*.

9.30 a.m. . . .

The man smiled to himself as the hot sud-scented water soothed keyed-in bitterness from his mind and body.

Happiness . . .

Happiness is a sponge, as big as a young football, with which to ease away bad memories, like wiping pus from a rotting wound. Happiness is steam, rising in clouds to a gloss-painted ceiling. Happiness is being clean, without the smell of carbolic. Happiness is the distant sound of Sinatra singing *The*

Tender Trap. Happiness is . . .

There was a knock on the bathroom door.

That, too, is happiness; a bathroom with a door, and the sudden realisation that, before anybody enters, they'll knock. Privacy. That, too, is happiness.

He called, 'C-come in.'

She had huge towels over one arm and a silk dressing-gown over the other. She kept her eyes averted, as she walked to the cork-seated chair, draped the dressing-gown across its back, then turned her back to him to arrange the towels along the heated rail.

As she fussed with the towels, she said, 'Your clothes. I've taken them from the wardrobe. They're on the bed, waiting.'

'D'you think they'll f-fit?'

'I think you might have to pull the belt in a notch or two.'

He slid deep into the sud-surfaced water then, after a pause, said, 'W-why don't you t-turn round?'

'I—er—I don't know what you mean.' She kept her back to him.

'L-look at me,' he said, simply.

Still with her hands on the towels, she breathed, 'I don't want to embarrass you.'

'W-what?'

'When you're ready. I'll be downstairs. Don't hurry . . . but, when you're ready.'

She hurried from the bathroom, without once glancing in his direction.

The man thought . . .

And that, too. My darling, you're not a fool. Nor do you think I'm a fool. To embarrass me? After what I've accepted as 'normal' for the last twelve years? You're not a child. Nor am I a child. To embarrass me? When we used to bath together, so often? When our around-the-house nudity was taken for granted.

In that respect you haven't changed. People like you grow more tolerant with the years. They don't turn into hypocrites. They don't censure more . . . they censure less.

To tell the truth. That's all I'm here for. To tell the truth, and hear the truth. No explosive re-awakening of passion. We're both civilised people. We both know. It isn't done that way . . . if it's done at all.

If it's done at all . . .

He soaked in the bath for another ten minutes, or so. Then he dried himself on soft, warm towels. He hesitated, then the ghost-smile touched his lips as he reached for the talc and patted a thin film of *French Almond* onto his skin. He tied the dressing-gown cord slightly around his waist and padded from the bathroom, along the corridor and into the master bedroom.

The clothes were there, on the bed. Fresh linen, socks, nylon shirt, his favourite tie and the ash-grey suit he'd always worn for special occasions. No off-the-peg suit, that. Bespoke-tailored, and trousers and jacket fit to be worn by a successful accountant out to meet and impress an important client. He reached down and fingered the cloth almost lovingly between thumb and forefinger. Beautiful material; the ultimate in the weaver's craft. Five fittings; he'd needed five fittings before the craftsman responsible for the creation of that suit had been satisfied with its 'hang', with the line-up of the lapels, with the smooth fit of the shoulders and with the under-arm snugness.

He turned and glanced at the dressing-table, with its full-width, tilted mirror. His hair-brushes were there, ready for use. And two freshly laundered handkerchiefs, each with his initials stitched in blue at one corner. And the moccasins; hand-made and of doe-skin . . . the most comfortable indoor footwear he'd ever owned.

The man thought . . .

You're trying hard, darling. Full marks, for effort. You're trying very hard, darling. A little too hard, perhaps. It's all a little too obvious . . .

(*The sergeant had joined the uniformed policeman at the public counter. The sergeant was as dogmatic—as immovable—as the P.C.*

'*It won't do, sir. It's gone ten o'clock. We can't just telephone a senior officer and tell him somebody wants to see him.*'

'*Why not?*'

'*He'll want a reason.*'

'*There is a reason.*'

The P.C. said, '*Yes, sir. But he'll want to* know *that reason.*'

'*We have cranks,*' *said the sergeant, bluntly.*

'*I'm not a crank.*'

'*No, sir . . . but, how do we know that?*'

'*Do I look like a crank?*'

The P.C. smiled, and said, '*You'd be surprised, sir. Few of 'em do.*'

'*Do I sound like a crank?*'

'*Frankly . . . yes,*' *growled the sergeant.*

'*You're not very helpful, sergeant. Neither of you are very helpful.*'

The sergeant chewed his lower lip in indecision, for a moment, then asked, '*Just, exactly, who do you want to see?*'

'*A senior officer. A senior detective, if possible.*'

'*Finney?*' *The P.C. made the suggestion to the sergeant.* '*Detective Chief Inspector Finney?*'

'*Try his home,*' *said the sergeant, reluctantly.* '*Tell him . . .*'

'*No!*'

'*What?*' *The sergeant's expression reflected his growing impatience.*

'*Not Finney . . . anybody, but Finney.*')

The woman touched the cutlery, the plates and the napkins, as she waited. It was something to do; something with which to occupy her nervous fingers.

It was ridiculous. To *be* afraid was ridiculous. To have a meal, like this—lobster salad, with trimmings and wine—at this hour of the day . . . *that* was ridiculous. Even Sinatra sounded faintly ridiculous, at this hour and in these circumstances.

She moved to the hi-fi equipment and notched the volume down a shade; *One More For The Road* became little more than a sad, slightly embittered, but still beautiful echo in an impeccably furnished room, the centre-piece of which was a dining table set out for the wrong sort of meal.

She returned to the table and stood, with the tips of her stiffened fingers resting on its polished surface.

Stupidity and nostalgia, carried to ridiculous lengths.

The woman thought . . .
Or, perhaps, lying carried to ridiculous lengths? Kindness? Simple humanity? Or, guilt? Does guilt come into it, somewhere? And, if it does, should there be guilt?

Damnation, this whole set-up is like something from a cheap Victorian romance. This is the tail-end of the twentieth century, for God's sake. People don't behave like this. Women don't behave like this . . . not unless it's a deliberate put-on.

A manuscript. If some cheap scribbler sent me a manuscript with this sort of situation—with this brand of honey-sweet dialogue—with this deliberately contrived set-up . . . damn it, it would be on its way back by return post.

It's not even good fiction.

So, how the hell can we live it out as fact?

9.45 a.m. . . .

'Again!' exploded Finney.

24

'Twice. Twice, in one night.'

The detective sergeant's name was Holmes. Stanley Holmes but, because policemen indulged themselves in a childish play of words, and because Holmes habitually signed his name 'S. Holmes', he was invariably known as 'Sherlock'. Holmes didn't mind. He'd grown used to it. He had a fury, all his own, but it was a fury which, for much of his life, he could readily control and, as he made the numerical correction to Finney's outraged exclamation, it was in a calm, unhurried tone. Bawling and shouting wasn't going to reduce 'twice' into 'once' . . . therefore, why bawl and shout?

'How many's that?' snarled Finney. 'Six?'

'Seven.'

'Seven . . . in less than a month.'

'The same comedian . . . obviously.'

'Obviously.'

'Same M.O. Same class of property. And always good class silver. Usually Georgian . . . with gold, if there's any around, and it doesn't have to be searched for.'

'Tell me something I don't know, sergeant,' grunted Finney. 'Tell me something I don't *dream* about.'

'I've checked with Crime Intelligence.'

'And?'

'Nothing . . . he's either an import, a new man at the game or somebody who's thought out a completely new angle.'

'And, that's all?'

'That's all.'

'For what good they do . . .' Finney snorted his disgust. 'Coppers, sat on their arse, all day. Filling in forms. Tooling around with filing systems. And they can tell us sod-all. What the hell *good* are they?'

Instead of answering a question which wasn't expecting an answer, Holmes said, 'Fingerprints and the Kodak boys are on the scene.'

'For what good *they'll* do.'

'Dogs are on their way.'

'They'll be cocking their legs up at every lamp-post . . . as usual.'

'And I've got three men on enquiries. With a couple of uniformed squad-car teams to help out with the ground-work.'

Finney dropped into one of the two swivel-chairs which the C.I.D. Office boasted. He thought and, as he thought, he frowned. Holmes waited for the master-mind to come up with some blinding solution.

In the main, Holmes was the sort of bloke who didn't indulge himself in violent likes or dislikes; life was too short for that brand of garbage. Finney was a detective chief inspector, which meant that Finney ordered and Holmes obeyed. Thus, the rules of the game. Obedience didn't necessarily equate with agreement, but rank (and the sort of man Finney was) precluded all serious argument. Okay, Finney was a slob, but he wasn't the only slob drawing police pay; come to that, he wasn't the only slob drawing detective allowance. They were around. And, if you had any gumption, you accepted 'em, worked alongside 'em and kept your opinions under lock and key.

And (fair play) Finney's brand of policing sometimes paid dividends. It was *dangerous,* but it sometimes worked. The growing problem was that each year more and more people objected to having a clenched fist waved around under their nose. Bish-bash bobbying had had its day . . . and, one fine morning, Finney would wake up to reality.

Till then . . .

'We're hitting it from the wrong end,' mused Finney.

'Think so.'

'Scores o' bloody questions. And nobody has any answers. Nobody ever *sees* anything.'

'If we don't ask the questions, we won't get the answers.'

'We're asking the wrong people.'

'So far,' agreed Holmes.

Finney hauled himself upright. He prowled the floor-space which separated the rows of paper-piled desks; hands deep in his trouser pockets, head pushed forward and jaw jutting as he continued.

'Georgian silverware.'

'And an odd gold trinket, here and there.'

'Seven bloody busts.'

'With the two reported this morning.'

'More than six thousand quid . . . right?'

'Today's two jobs—an estimate, so far . . . but, six thousand. That, at least.'

'A thousand quid a trip. That's not bad going, sergeant.'

'It pays . . . until he's caught.'

'*If* he's caught.'

Holmes didn't reply.

Finney said, 'Who the hell takes that sort of stuff?'

'Somebody. He must *have* a customer. We've circulated all the local jewellers, silversmiths and . . .'

'And *they*, of course,' interrupted Finney, harshly, 'will co-operate. Especially if one of 'em happens to be the bloody fence. He'll be the *first* to co-operate.'

'What else?' asked Holmes, sadly.

'Let's suppose a few things,' growled Finney. 'Let's suppose a few things we can take for granted. Then, suppose a few more things that are more likely than not. There's a fence . . . right?'

'Unless he's a keen collector.'

'Don't let us be too funny-funny, sergeant,' warned Finney.

'A fence,' agreed Holmes, mildly.

'But it's going to be melted down. That, for a cert. Every piece is hallmarked and identifiable. Some of 'em have even been photographed, for the insurance files. As they are, he can't get rid . . . whoever buys 'em. So, he had to melt 'em down into ingots—bars—what the hell shape happens to take his fancy. Then *used*. As basic metal silver.'

'Unless *he* sells,' suggested Holmes.

'No. That's too dangerous.' Finney stopped his pacing, leaned his backside against a desk edge, stared across at Holmes, and said, 'Fences. They're chary bastards. This one—whoever he is—handles identifiable silverware. Good stuff. Some of it, near-antique. Now, he knows damn well he can't sell it, as it is. Which lowers *his* price . . . old ballock-brains, who's doing all the lifting, *he* won't be getting seven thousand quid for his bits and pieces. He'll be lucky if he gets half that. Because it's all going into a melting-pot, somewhere. Which, unless it's stamped and assay-marked, makes it even *more* bloody dangerous. You don't pay for the groceries, at the nearest supermarket, with a home-made silver bar . . . right?'

Holmes nodded.

Finney continued, 'You can sell it . . . to some other bent bastard. But that means *trusting* somebody. Your own kind, maybe. But fences don't have trusting natures . . . that's why they live so long. On the other hand, you can *use* it. If you have the equipment. If you're authorised to work in silver.'

'A silver-smith.'

'A little bit here. A little bit there. Buy the normal amount of legit metal. Keep the books neat. But—y'know . . . mix it among. That way, the legit stuff goes further. The non-legit stuff comes cheap. You can get *really* competitive, in the price-tags. You get paid for the fenced stuff, via the back door . . . and nobody can prove a damn thing.'

'Nobody can prove a damn thing,' echoed Holmes, softly.

'Except . . .'

Holmes waited.

'Except,' mused Finney, 'until it *is* used, it's *there*. Locked away somewhere. Maybe already melted down. But there!

Silver that shouldn't be around. Silver you shouldn't even *have*. All we have to do is find the bloody stuff.'

'Is that all?' Mild amusement rode Holmes's tone.

'Silver-smiths,' said Finney, harshly. 'They don't come a penny a dozen. Here, in Bordfield . . . how many, would you say?'

'Twenty,' guessed Holmes. 'No more than twenty.'

'And one of 'em on the twist.'

'*If* it's Bordfield.'

'My money says Bordfield.' Finney was his usual dogmatic self. 'Why *not* Bordfield?'

'Shitting on your own doorstep?' suggested Holmes.

'But we look prize twats if it *is* Bordfield, and we haven't checked.'

'Agreed.'

'So-o . . . we'll stick to Bordfield. Right?'

Holmes nodded.

Finney resumed his pacing, between the desks.

He said, 'First things first. Snouts. Not the bad farts who talk for the sake of talking. Somebody who might know— somebody who *will* know . . . and we squeeze a couple of arias out of him.'

Holmes said, 'We've been round the snouts.'

'And nobody knows anything?'

'Nobody knows anything,' agreed Holmes.

'Pure, driven slush?'

'If they know, they aren't talking.'

'Not quite the same thing, sergeant. Not *quite* the same thing.'

Holmes sighed.

'Page.' Finney stopped, less than a yard from Holmes, met him eye for eye, and said, 'How does Page grab you?'

'Inky Page?'

'The one and only.'

'Page is straight, these days.'

'Come *on,* sergeant. They just *don't.'*

'Ten years?' said Holmes and, for the first time, real disagreement was in his voice.

'He hasn't been *convicted* in the last ten years . . . that's all.'

'He hasn't even been *suspected.'*

'By you, maybe. But, by me . . . I suspect the bastards for the rest of their lives.'

Holmes compressed his lips, but remained silent.

'Inky Page,' said Finney. 'A great one for nicking jewellery.'

'Watches,' corrected Holmes.

'What the hell are watches, if they're not jewellery?'

'They're not silverware.'

'They're sold over the same counter, sergeant. Page was a warehouse thief. He helped himself to timepieces. Some—we know—he sold to people in pubs. The usual crap. But, a hell of a lot . . . Who knows? We never found out. They were never recovered.'

'He did his time,' said Holmes, flatly. 'He came out . . . and he's been straight, ever since.'

'Knackers!'

Holmes moved his shoulders.

'He has pals,' said Finney.

'Don't we all?'

'Slimy types, who can't keep their fingers to themselves.'

'Occasionally.'

'*Caught*, occasionally.'

'He's nobody's keeper. Nobody ever is.'

'Judas Priest!' Finney raised his eyes to the ceiling. 'What bloody innocence. What unqualified charity . . . and from a man who should have seen it *all*. Take the nipple out of your mouth, Holmes. Stop sucking pap, look around you and see the workings of this beautiful, high-stinking world. Page is a crook. His pals are all crooks. He lives surrounded by bent bleeders . . . therefore, he *knows.* He keeps his trap zipped, because he's also surrounded by puce-brained pillucks who all think he's such a nice guy. A reformed character. Next in line to be Archbishop of York, maybe. He don't know nothin', because he won't *tell* nothin'. Ain't that beautiful, sergeant? Don't you think that's really beautiful? From where *he* stands, I mean.'

'Meaning,' said Holmes, flatly, 'that you're going to—er—question, Inky Page.'

'*We* are going to question him.' Finney's teeth showed in an anticipatory grin. 'Okay—*I* am going to question him . . . while you stand by, ready to swear I never laid a glove on him. Strictly speaking, I'm going to kick his goolies all the way up to his throat, unless he has answers to every damn question I throw at him. C'mon . . . I'll drive.'

9.50 a.m. . . .

From across the table, she watched him fork the salad into his mouth, chew it slowly and carefully, swallow, then dab his lips with the napkin before he moistened his mouth with the wine.

So different. So changed. Each action a meticulously executed movement from an almost-forgotten discipline. Like a man, bed-ridden for years, taking the first steps in the re-learning of his natural act of walking. This husband of hers who, twelve years ago, had had such confidence; who could sit at a banquet table—who could attend any function, however 'official'—who could walk into the best restaurant in the land, and be confronted by the most exotic dishes, served by eagle-eyed waiters—and *always* do the 'right thing', naturally and without apparent thought.

And, now this.

He didn't fumble. That would have been too much. But the

31

tiny pause, between each separate sequence in the conveyance of food, or drink, to his mouth, hurt her like a stab of physical pain; he was 'remembering'; like Sinatra, he was 'note perfect' but, unlike Sinatra, the tempo was all wrong. There was no natural flow. The very concentration needed to prevent 'mistakes' was making the simple act of eating contrived and unnatural.

She murmured, 'Easy, darling. Just relax . . . it's all over.'

He glanced across the table at her, the fork paused half-way to his lips, and his eyes told her how monumentally wrong she was.

It was not 'all over' . . . it would never be 'all over'.

Sinatra . . .

She suddenly realised how much like Sinatra he looked. Not the grey hair, but the face and the build. The old Sinatra; the Sinatra who'd fought Crosby for top placing in the affections of the kids. The bean-stalk Sinatra; lean-cheeked and hollow-eyed; the *Nancy With The Laughing Face* Sinatra; the youngster who'd just parted company with the Dorsey band, and was out to warble his way into musical history . . . long before the 'Ol' Blue Eyes' tag was invented.

The track on the hi-fi changed, and Sinatra's voice came in after the immaculate intro. *It's Always You.* Bouncy—happy . . . but with that hint of bitterness which no other voice in the world carried.

The tears were near enough to sting her eyes.

The meal—this meal—had been all wrong. For all the right reasons, she'd done all the wrong things.

The woman thought . . .
Why? In God's name, why? What made me think I could play-act this thing out? What made me think I could turn back the clock, replace the pages on the calendar? Make twelve years do a disappearing trick?

We're strangers. We don't know each other any more. We aren't married any more.

All this. This is pure self-indulgence. Why don't I stop kidding myself? I have a stranger in my house, a stranger eating at my table, and even though I have documentary proof that this stranger is also my husband, he's still a stranger. He's still a stranger!

A magnificent stranger. Strong . . . but with a peculiar and terrifying strength alien to the physical strength of my husband. A gentle strength. A strength of character. A strength of self-discipline. The strength of a stranger who frightens me a little.

I could love him. I swear—I could, so easily, love this stranger. But not the same love. Not the old love. The love of a slave, or the love of a mother. But, not the love of a wife.

A shop-soiled love . . . which, with kindness and with understanding, he'd reject.

So, why offer it? Why hurt him even more than he's already been hurt?

Why? In God's name, why? Why did I think up this terrible charade?

The man said, 'How's the b-business going?'

'The—er . . . ' She blinked her thoughts from her mind and forced her concentration upon small-talk.

'The b-business? Th-the agency?'

'Fine. Fine. Every month a little better.'

'G-good.' He paused, and went through the rigmarole of lifting food to his mouth, chewing, swallowing, raising the napkin, then touching his lips with the wine. He said, 'I'd have th-thought there w-wasn't much c-call, up north, here.'

'On the contrary.'

'Oh?'

'You'd be surprised.'

'R-really?'

'There's a lot of talent up here.'

'P-people who th-think they can write?'

'People who *can* write.' She felt an upsurge of confidence. The conversation was moving into something about which she could talk with certainty. Her pet subject. She said, 'Look—reputable literary agencies . . . about half a dozen outside London. No more. And they're all in the Home Counties. Oh, yes . . . one in Scotland. But, that's all. Every other agency's in London. Now, why the hell should that be so? Why *London*? Why not scattered around the country . . . with contacts with London-based agencies. Like mine.

'By, and large, northerners don't *like* London. They're parochial . . . All right . . . ridiculously parochial. They don't completely *trust* Londoners. It's silly. It's illogical. But it's *there*, and nobody's going to alter it, so why not make use of it? Why not do everybody a good turn?'

'And m-make money,' he murmured.

'Is that wrong?'

'N-n-no. I d-didn't say . . .'

'I charge the ten per-cent. Like the London crowd. I know a handful of editors from some of the main publishing houses. I've made it my business to *get* to know them. And they know *me*. They knew me well enough to read—to at least *read*—whatever I send them. They know *I* think it's worth reading.'

'And the authors th-think you do it all with m-mirrors.'

'The authors are dealing with somebody from their own neck of the woods. They're happy. How it's done doesn't interest them. That it's done from up here . . . *that's* what counts.'

'Look.' She leaned forward, slightly, all unease gone in her enthusiasm. 'We get manuscripts. Scores. Hundreds a week, sometimes. A lot of it's crappy. My God! You should see what some people call "writing". But some of it . . . it shows promise and, if the writer's prepared to accept advice, there's

34

a fifty-fifty chance of acceptance. Occasionally, we get a pearl. A natural. And, when that happens, it's all been worth waiting for. Northern writing, from a northern writer, who probably wouldn't have trusted his work with a Londoner. We have about half a dozen . . . and, for them, alone, it's been worth creating the agency.'

He was smiling across the table at her. That slow, spectral smile; compound of sadness, bitterness, nostalgia and . . . something else. Something she couldn't identify.

He said, 'S-six authors. G-good. They must do w-well for you.'

'I'm sorry.' She leaned back in her chair and moved her shoulders in a tiny shrug.

'Why?'

'I tend to be carried away . . . that's all.'

'N-no.' He shook his head, in a kindly gesture. 'I'm interested. B-but six authors. It d-doesn't seem many. Not for success.'

'They're the foundation stones.' She watched his face; tried to detect real interest in this topic of conversation. 'The rest . . . three, or four, books. That's all. Sometimes only one. We represent a lot of writers . . . writers, not *authors*. Men, and women, who have a book in them. Perhaps two books. Sometimes people who are experts in a certain field.' She smiled at the recollection, then said, 'One man wrote a book on heraldry. Coats of arms . . . that sort of thing. He'd had ten rejections. We placed it, within a month . . . and with a good publishing house. It was a well-written book. But he'd been sending it to all the wrong publishers . . . as simple as *that*. He thinks we're magicians. We're not. It's merely that our job is to know which publisher is likely to be even *interested* in a book on heraldry.'

'W-we?'

The hesitation was barely noticeable, before she said, 'Three of us. We work as a team. We share a secretary and girl Friday. We each supposedly "specialise". Children's books. Romantic novels. Adventure and crime. We don't *really* specialise . . . but we try to. We have one thing in common. We can recognise decent writing . . . we hope.'

The man thought . . .
Why can't she tell me? Is it so difficult to speak a name? Is she so afraid? So ashamed? So unwilling to tell the truth?

(The wall-clock, beyond the public counter, showed fifteen minutes after ten o'clock. From the interior of the police station a bell rang; it rang with the double signal of a telephone bell, but it was no ordinary telephone-bell ring. It was loud and urgent. It caused the heads of the uniformed sergeant and police constable to jerk, momentarily, towards whence it came.

The sergeant snapped, 'I'll take it,' and hurried away from the counter.

The P.C. looked uncomfortable, and said, 'Look, sir, we can't waste time . . .'

'You're not wasting time.'

'We've other things to do. Important things.'

'This is important.'

The P.C. compressed his lips, reached a decision, then said, 'Okay. But you'll have to wait.'

'I'm quite prepared to wait.'

As he lifted the flap of the counter, the P.C. said, 'Come with me, please. Number Three Interview Room. It's just down the corridor. You can wait there.')

Finney could drive. However else he could be faulted (and he *could* be faulted, in many things) his handling of a motor car was a poem of co-ordinated movements. A poem, one of those galloping poems—one of those How-They-Brought-The-Good-

36

News poems—which zip along, without pause, and leave the reader breathless and heart-pounding. But, a poem, nevertheless.

He was, of course, police-trained . . . but that didn't always mean too much. But, with Finney, it meant something; it meant technical perfection married to a natural genius. In this force, nobody argued about who was *best* driver . . . only about who was *second*-best.

Nevertheless, Holmes worried.

The driving didn't worry him. Finney threaded the Merc. through the city traffic with the sure touch of a master-basket-maker weaving cane; he knew, to within an inch, where and when the Merc. could slip ahead and, more than that, he seemed to have an uncanny knowledge of what every other vehicle on the road was going to do; he was accelerating for gaps, before the gaps appeared. Holmes marvelled at the driving, but worried about what might come *after* the driving.

'Linkwood Park . . . eh?'

'I reckon,' agreed Holmes.

'If not, they'll know where he's working.'

Holmes suppressed a sigh.

Harry 'Inky' Page didn't know what was coming at him. And Inky was straight. Holmes was sure of this. Ten years ago, Inky had walked away from prison, having paid his debt to society and, since that day, he hadn't put a foot wrong. As far as Holmes was concerned, those ten years proved it; not even a hint . . . nothing! Inky was one of the minority who had sense enough to learn. The system couldn't be licked; any more sticky-finger-work and he'd be back inside again.

Inky had at least *that* much gumption.

But, because of his refusal to deny prolonged friendship, poor old Inky was a betwixt-and-between type. *He* was straight . . . but some of his pals still corkscrewed around. Stupid. You turn your back on a way of life, and you turn your back on

37

the men and women who were part of that life. If you *didn't*
... There was always a 'Finney' around. There was always
somebody who could see fire where there wasn't even smoke.

Holmes murmured, 'Give him a chance.'

'Eh?'

'Inky. Don't be too rough. Give him a chance.'

'A *choice*, sergeant. You know me. I *always* give them a
straight choice ... they talk, or they bleed.'

10.10 a.m. ...

The woman said, 'Coffee?'

'L-later ... if you don't mind.'

'Cigarette?'

'Th-thanks.'

'Ol' Blue Eyes' was doing his unique nut on *The Lady Is A
Tramp* as she held out the case, and he took a cigarette; as she
flicked a throw-away lighter and held the flame first to his
cigarette, then to her own; as she carefully positioned the
heavy glass ash-tray, handy for both of them.

The meal had been ... a success?

It had staved off the inevitable; to *that* extent it had been
a success. It had been something in the nature of a 'stay of
execution', however temporary; to *that* extent it had been a
success.

But, they couldn't eat forever.

And these cigarettes ... they were merely an extension of
the meal.

She groped around in her mind, seeking some safe topic of
conversation.

She drew hard on her cigarette, then said, 'What was it
like?'

'W-what?'

'Prison. What was it like?'

'Oh?'

'No! Don't tell me.' She waved an impatient and apologetic hand. 'I shouldn't have asked. It's—it's thoughtless of me. Please . . . I'm sorry.'

'I-it stank,' he said, simply.

'No. I really shouldn't have . . .'

'It was d-degrading.' Life seemed to flicker at the back of his eyes, for the first time. He continued, 'W-why shouldn't you ask? W-why shouldn't you be curious? I don't mind. I'll t-tell you.'

'No! It was just something . . .'

'W-when I say it "stank", I'm not using the word as a c-colloquialism. It really does. Prisons *stink*. Th-they have a smell of their own. Half disinfectant, half body-filth. Public baths and public lavatories. The worst, from both . . . that's what "prison smell" is l-like. You get used to it. It's amazing, really. You really do get used to it. You don't notice it any more . . . after a few months. Twelve years. I wasn't even *aware*.' He frowned anxiously, then asked, 'I-it isn't, is it?'

'What?'

'With me? The smell. It isn't *still* there, is it?'

'Oh, my God!' she breathed.

'Truthfully?' He was like a child; eager for reassurance. 'I don't know. To me, it's . . . natural. But, honestly, *is* it?'

'No, darling, it isn't,' she whispered. 'Not a trace. I swear.'

'G-good.' The ghost-smile brushed his lips, and he was satisfied. He said, 'That's the first thing you get used to, you see. The smell. The atmosphere. Like stables, I suppose. Like kennels. The other things . . . some of them, you n-never get used to.'

He paused, to draw on his cigarette then, almost musingly, he continued, 'R-rapists have a bad time, at first. Especially ch-child rapists. For the first year, or so. There was hardly a day when I didn't hurt . . . somewhere. Usually in the genitals. I was kicked. Kneed. Everything. And, in the stomach . . . there, too. Not often on the face . . . but sometimes. An occasional black eye. That sort of thing.'

She looked shocked, and said, 'I thought warders weren't . . .'

'No—not warders . . . fellow-prisoners. They're very p-puritanical, you know. The criminal classes. Murder. They'll tolerate murder quite happily. Especially if it's "justified" . . . if *they* think it's "justified". I-I've known them have a sort of "welcoming committee" waiting. Ready to congratulate the man convicted. Things are made easy for him, from the start. But, anything to do with kids. Or with your mother. Suppose you knock your mother about . . . however much of a cow she is. Or your sister. That sort of thing. They have their own scale of evil. It's not our scale. It's not a "civilised" scale . . . not to the outside world. B-but it's *their* scale. And it's *their* world.'

'But . . .' What he was saying fascinated her. It was a fascination bordering upon the morbid, but she couldn't help herself. She said, 'The warders. Surely they can . . .'

'The screws.' He held the cigarette upright, in front of his eyes. 'That's more important than the screws. Tobacco. Tobacco controls a prison . . . not the screws. The screws make sure the inmates are fed and watered. That's all. After that, they're an extension of the wall. An extension of the bars. They make sure the two worlds never meet. The inside world and the outside world. But, they don't control. The block bosses control. Through fear. Through bribery. Through tobacco. *They* control. *They* decide who's going to be punished. What the punishment will be. Whether, or not, there'll be a riot. It's their world—that world . . . and *they're* kings.'

Something—the sheer intensity of his words, at a guess— had beaten the slight stammer which had entered his speech since last they'd met. Since that time, twelve years back, when she'd seen him for a few moments in a police cell. She noticed ... and she wondered.

He inhaled cigarette smoke, then said, 'Kings depart. New kings take over. And the n-new kings either don't know, or don't care. The last few years it was easier. I wasn't hated as m-much.'

The man thought ...
Why the hell am I telling her? Why the hell am I torturing myself, by trying to explain? The pain ... who can remember pain? It makes you scream but, within days, you can't remember, you can't explain. You can't describe. So, why the hell am I trying?

She screwed out her cigarette, stood up, and said, 'I'll see to the coffee. Be—er—comfortable. We'll have it in the arm-chairs, if you like.'

He nodded, and she hurried away, towards the kitchen.

In the kitchen, she wept quietly as she prepared the coffee. She wept at so many things. At memories. At cruelties already committed, and cruelties yet to come. She wept at the wreck of a man; a man who had once been a complete man but a man who, over the last dozen years, had been gutted and debased until he was little more than a polite, performing animal. And she wept, too, because the division between love and sympathy was so blurred—so indistinct ... therefore, she wasn't *sure*.

Myra Finney also wept. Her weeping was an internal thing; a secret thing of which even she herself was only vaguely aware.

She still wore her soiled house-coat and torn nightdress. Her hair was still bird's-nest bedraggled. She still slopped around the house in her mules, and the pop music on the transistor was back at full volume.

Yet, in her own way, she wept.

Despite outward appearances, she was a woman who had once been an attractive woman and now, not yet thirty, she was a hag . . . and, *because* she was a woman, she knew it. She couldn't cook; nobody had taught her to cook; the mock-ease with which cookery books described this art was, to her, a con trick because they all pre-supposed a basic knowledge she lacked; evening classes were out of the question, because the kids demanded every evening of her life; afternoon-classes were equally out of the question, because her husband was equally demanding that, at whatever time he arrived home, she be waiting with a meal ready . . . and yet she couldn't *cook*! Each impossibility was equally impossible, therefore she'd *never* learn to cook.

Tidiness was not of her nature. The scattering of books, magazines and newspapers was something she didn't notice. Dusting and polishing bored her to distraction. She loved the clean feel of stepping from a hot bath; but the messing about of preparation, and the dreary chore of cleaning the bath, and clearing the bathroom, *after* the bath was too much trouble to make it more than a weekly ritual.

She used cosmetics much as an unskilled house-painter uses paint; to mask the faults and to provide a temporary façade. Again, she had never been *taught*. She had never taken the trouble to *learn*. Her text-books on the application of make-up were the glossies; the adverts, where symmetry was guyed up by experts to give the impression of normality made beautiful.

She was a sucker for give-away gimmickry. She was God's gift to the T.V. ad-men. Every check-out girl in the local supermarket knew her by her first name.

She was a female slob, and she knew it, but she tried to drive that knowledge out via never-ending raucous pop music played at full blast; as if this non-melodic noise might, in some way, cover up then wipe clean, her own shortcomings.

It didn't.

She knew it never would.

Therefore, she wept deep inside herself . . . even though she was not aware of the weeping.

Ralph Finney didn't weep. Ralph Finney *never* wept.

He said, 'Page. We'd like a word with him.'

The head gardener said, 'He finishes at twelve. Half-day, Saturday.'

'We can't wait till twelve.'

'Oh, aye?' The head gardener was an elderly man; a man blessed with the solid patience essential for his craft. He was prepared to be convinced . . . but not hustled. He said, 'Urgent, is it?'

'We think so.'

The head gardener dug a broken cherry-wood from the pocket of his apron, clamped his teeth around the mouthpiece and tested it for draught.

'So, where do we find him?' demanded Finney.

'Here . . . at twelve o'clock. He'll be knocking off, then.'

'Now?' snapped Finney.

'Depends.' The head gardener brought matches from the pocket of his apron.

'Old man,' warned Finney, 'don't play silly buggers. Be advised.'

'*Young* man.' The head gardener scratched a match into flame, held it to the bowl of the cherry-wood and spoke between puffs of smoke from thin twist. 'Don't use bad language at me. I'm old enough to be your father.'

'What the hell . . .'

'Uhu!' The head gardener raised warning eyebrows. 'Any man who can't talk without swearing has a poor command of English. Didn't anybody ever tell you that?'

'We'd like to ask Mr. Page a few questions,' said Holmes, gently.

43

'That's right. *Mister* Page,' echoed Finney, harshly.

'What about?'

Finney said, 'Well, not gardening . . . that for sure.'

'He could tell you a thing or two. He's not a bad gardener.'

'Look—for Christ's sake!—what's all the . . .'

'These men are paid.' The head gardener spoke through a haze of tobacco smoke. 'Local rates . . . that's what pays 'em. One of my jobs is to make sure the rate-payers aren't swindled. If it's urgent . . . all right. But, if it isn't urgent, you'll have to wait.'

'It's urgent,' snarled Finney.

Holmes said, 'It's about theft. Big theft.'

The head gardener frowned.

'We think he can help us,' continued Holmes. 'We don't think *he* did it. Don't get the wrong idea. He's honest—we've no reason to think Page is dishonest . . . but we think he can help.'

'If he's a thief . . .'

'No! We don't think *he's* a thief.'

'. . . I want to know.'

'We'll let you know,' said Finney. 'When we've seen him. When we've questioned him. We'll let you know.'

The head gardener nodded, and said, 'I'll be here, waiting.'

'Right . . . where is he?'

'The other side of the pond. With the flag irises. He's dividing the biggest clumps. Tell him I sent you.'

'Where can we talk to him?'

'I've already told you. He's at . . .'

'In private.'

'Oh!' The head gardener paused for a moment, then said, 'The fern-house. Tell him. Tell him to take you to the fern-house . . . that I said so. And, when you've finished, come back here. I'll be waiting. I want no thieves on my staff.'

'I've already told you. He isn't . . .'

'C'mon, sergeant. Let's see the germ.'

As they hurried along the tarmac path, Finney grumbled, 'Ever noticed? They're all the bloody same. Make 'em top dog, and they think they're special. Him! Chief constable of the bloody weeds . . . they're all the same.'

10.30 a.m. . . .

The man placed his coffee cup carefully onto the glass-covered surface of the occasional table, and said, 'S-sex.'

It was such a soft-spoken word, and yet it was like the chisel-end of a ripping-bar inserted into the crack of rotting woodwork. It was the first tiny act of destruction; the first step towards shifting something she was terrified of removing.

She waited. She tried to control her breathing; not to pant, as if after a long and hurried walk.

He raised his head and met her eyes with his own lifeless eyes, and said, 'C-can we talk about it?'

'Er—sex?' she breathed.

'Twelve years in prison makes it v-very important. D-disproportionately important, perhaps.'

'I—er—I see.'

'Without women.'

'Of course.'

'It's—it's unnatural. And one unnatural thing l-leads to other un-unnatural things. It's only to b-be expected.'

'Obviously.'

'After tobacco . . . *that's* the most important thing.'

'Sex?'

'Un-natural sex. Th-the only sex available. Th-that and masturbation.'

'Look, I think . . .'

'Yes! We *should* t-talk about it.'

'If you must,' she sighed. 'It isn't important . . . really. What

45

happened *isn't* important. That you're home, again. That's the only thing that's important.'

'So wrong.' He shook his head slowly and with infinite sadness. 'Twelve years . . . unimportant? Th-that's foolish talk. It can't be *not* important. I-it's changed you. It's changed me. I-it has to have done.'

She took a deep breath, then whispered, 'If you wish.'

'Th-they have "wives". They *call* them "wives". F-first "g-girl friends", then "wives". T-to you—to ordinary people—it's disgusting. The courtship . . . there's a real courtship. Y-you have my word. P-presents. Tobacco, again . . . usually t-tobacco. Sometimes other things. T-toilet paper. I-imagine t-taking a girl you hope to m-marry the gift of a toilet-roll. A soft t-toilet roll . . .'

'Stop it!' she breathed.

'. . . Or t-toothpaste. N-not a whole tube . . . a half-used tube. A n-new razor-blade. Gifts. C-courting gifts. N-not chocolates, or flowers, or j-jewellery. Instead . . . a t-toilet roll. Something like th-that.'

'Please,' she pleaded, softly. 'I don't want to *know*.'

'Then the j-jealousies.' He was talking *at* her, not *to* her. That she had to listen didn't seem to interest him. He continued, 'Th-those jealousies. My God! I-I've seen one of the "g-girls" taunt two men to m-madness. Not once. M-many times. Blood s-spilled. Men m-marked for life. Eyes g-gouged. Sh-shivs—home-made shivs—sh-sharp as razors and used to c-carve the other s-suitor to the bone. And th-then, when it's all over, th-the "girl" embracing the winner. K-kissing. G-groping at each other, in front of the g-grinning . . .'

'*Stop it!*' Her near-scream seemed to jerk him from his reverie. She clenched her fists on the skirt covering the tops of her thighs, and pleaded, 'Please . . . no more. It's finished. It's over. No more.'

'Y-you don't want to know?' He sounded mildly surprised.

46

'I don't give a damn,' she said softly. Urgently. 'Understand me. I do not give a *damn*. If you had to turn "gay" . . . that doesn't matter. Homosexuality. I don't understand it. But, I don't condemn it. I do *not* condemn it.'

The look of surprise turned to shock.

Then, the wraith-smile flickered across his mouth, he lifted the coffee-cup and saucer from the occasional table, sipped, then said, 'Did I s-say *that*?'

'What?'

'Th-that I'd turned homosexual?'

'By—by implication. I thought you were trying to . . .'

'No.' He shook his head, slowly.

'Oh!'

'The conditions, inside prison. Th-that's all. What it's *like*. P-people. Don't know. People don't even *care*. B-but they should. Not the d-do-gooders. The "official visitors" . . . they don't help. Th-they're a joke. They don't c-count. But ordinary p-people. Whey they say, "He deserved it", or "They should have given him more" . . . d-do they *know* what they're say-ing? Not just being locked away. Th-that's bad enough . . . but that's *n-nothing*. It's—it's the other things. The foul things. The—the n-non-human things. *That's* the real punish-ment.' He paused then, in a faraway voice, touched with bitterness, continued, 'L-like me. Eighteen years, for r-rape. Eighteen! T-twelve, with remission for good behaviour. I w-wonder . . . did that judge *know*? It was a s-savage sentence. Even some of the screws . . . they were sh-shocked. T-ten. I *expected* ten. There'd—there'd been . . . the g-girl who'd b-been murdered by the m-man who'd given her a lift. You won't remember. B-but that's what did it.' The faint, goblin-grin came, and went, as he continued, 'Th-that's British justice . . . isn't it. You're p-punished for things you haven't done. An outraged public demands it. You're the *s-second*— or the *th-third* . . . and it has to be stopped. The previous ones

47

have n-nothing to do with you. Th-they're not your fault. But you're punished for *them*, as well. Th-the judge thought he was being a p-public benefactor. Was he? I—I d-don't know. D-did it stop hitch-hiking? H-hasn't anybody th-thumbed a lift, since? H-hasn't any other girl been m-molested? Th-that's what it was meant to do . . . that eighteen-year sentence. B-but —b-but if it *didn't* . . .'

Suddenly, he stopped talking and dropped his chin to his chest for a moment. As if he'd run out of words. As if he'd been drained dry of all argument; all logic; all pleading.

He raised his head, sipped at the cooling coffee, and his eyes were as lifeless as ever.

The woman thought . . .

He'll never get over it. He'll never recover. Ever! However much love. However much understanding. No matter what anybody does.

For the rest of his life, he's going to hold the world at arm's length. He's been debased too far. Degraded too often. He's suffered far too long, ever to return.

And yet . . .

He's my husband. He needs me now, more than he ever needed me. More than he ever needed anybody. Not to love— not merely to love—but to shelter behind. To use as a shield, against the world.

'Till death do us part' . . . oh my God!

He needs me, so desperately.

And I'm frightened of him. God forgive me, I'm frightened of him.

(He squashed his third cigarette into the tin ash-tray, on the table of Number Three Interview Room.

Three cigarettes—thirty cigarettes—it didn't matter. He could wait. They'd get to him, eventually. Meanwhile, the tubular-steel chair was comfortable enough. The room was light and airy, and almost clinically clean.

He could wait. If necessary, he could wait forever.)

The fern-house gave Holmes the creeps. It was like Burma; he'd never *been* to Burma, but he'd seen movies and read books. This dank, sweaty atmosphere—like Burma . . . any minute, a Jap sniper would take a pot-shot at them from somewhere in the gloom.

It was a moderately large, lean-to greenhouse, with the glass darkened with colour-wash, with the heat turned up past the seventy mark and with pools of rock-rimmed water to provide the stifling humidity. The rocks, around the pools, were thick with moss and algae, and the umpteen varieties of fern grew thick and luxuriant—fat and juicy—and some almost reached shoulder-height.

It was a creepy place . . . and it gave Holmes the creeps.

Page stood, mute, on the centre, concrete-surfaced path. He still wore his gardening apron and heavy, gardening boots. A very ordinary man. Average height, average build, average everything. Even as a crook he'd been no more than 'average' . . . which meant he always got caught. Until (having an average mentality) he'd seen the error of his way; the stupidity of spending hunks of his life divorced from the rest of mankind. Since then, he'd gone straight.

Holmes was ready to stake his life on it . . . that Page *was* straight.

Finney was standing with his back to Page, gazing at a gargantuan mass of foliage, beyond a scum-topped pool.

Finney was saying, 'Before we start, Page. I've read Hans Anderson. The brothers Grimm . . . I know 'em off by heart. All the "Noddy" books. You name the fairy story, Page—I know it . . . especially the one about "the man in the pub". Keep that in mind, and we'll get along fine. The sergeant,

49

here, tells me you've joined the good guys now. Me? I take a little more convincing. Inky Page—the bent bastard . . . you're still *that*, as far as I'm concerned. You getting all this?'

Page murmured, 'Yes, Mr. Finney.'

'Good.' Finney nodded approval at the mass of ferns. 'Because somebody is lifting silver in this town. Good silver. Georgian stuff . . . *that* good. Often, and a lot of it. Which, by the rules of this little parlour game, means there's a taker.' He paused then, softly, asked, 'Who's the taker, Page?'

'The fence?' added Holmes.

'I dunno, Mr. Finney, sir.'

Page was scared. That an ordinary, upright citizen wouldn't have been scared cut no ice. That Page *was*, at this time, an ordinary, upright citizen cut no ice. The ice-cutting came from the past; from the certainty that, as far as Finney was concerned, the past was also the present . . . plus the knowledge that Finney was *Finney*.

'I'll ask you a second time, Page,' murmured Finney. 'You've had your quota of garbage . . . remember that. Who's the fence?'

'If you know . . .' encouraged Holmes.

'I dunno, Mr. Finney. I swear . . .'

Finney turned. He did a left-about-turn, at speed; he spun on the heel of his left shoe and the sole of his right and, as he turned he fisted his left hand and brought it up in a vicious swipe. The back of the clenched fist ripped across Page's lips, and Page staggered back, caught his foot against one of the rocks and sprawled among the ferns.

Finney stared down at him.

In a flat, expressionless voice, he said, 'Don't damage the plants, Page. Your gaffer will tell you . . . rate-payers pay for those plants.'

'For Christ's sake! If you know anything,' said Holmes, and his voice was a little unsteady.

'I don't.' Page was near to tears. He wiped the back of a hand against his lips and smeared the trickle of blood. 'What d'you wanna do that for, Mr. Finney? If I knew anything . . .'

'Get up, Page.'

'No!' Page shook his head, violently.

'Up on your feet, germ.' Finney balanced himself on the balls of his feet, threateningly.

'You'll—you'll knock me down, again.'

'Very likely.'

'I—I ain't gonna get up, to be . . .'

'You prefer being kicked in the balls, in a prone position. That it?'

Page pushed himself to his feet. He held his arms in front of his face as a puny protection; cowering, as he waited for the next blow. He knew Finney. He knew Finney's reputation, and he was breathless with terror.

'Nice,' growled Finney. 'Very thoughtful. That gives me a clear swing at your guts.'

'Please, Mr. Finney. *Please!*'

Holmes said, 'You used a fence, Inky. Years back, you used a fence.'

From behind his arms, Page nodded.

'Who?'

'I ain't used him for years, Mr. Holmes.'

'Who did you use?'

'Honest. I'm . . .'

'*Who?*' snapped Finney.

'He's a . . . He's a jeweller.'

'Well, I never!' sneered Finney. 'A jeweller. A frigging *jeweller*. And, all this time, we've been thinking you've been selling hot watches to a bloody chemist.'

Holmes stepped forward a couple of paces. He deliberately positioned himself between Finney and the quaking Page.

'Put your arms down, Inky,' he said, gently.

51

Page hesitated. He peeped from behind his forearms, then slowly lowered his hands to his sides.

Holmes said, 'Inky, you know me. You know Chief Inspector Finney. And, for your own sake, I hope you know we mean business. Somebody's putting good silver away. Ten years back . . . the boy who took your watches may have moved up a few notches. These days, he might be handling silver. If not *he* might know something. Come to that, *you* might know something . . . I mean the lifter, not the receiver. Something. Anything. We're greedy for a lead, Inky. I'll tell you *how* greedy . . . so listen. Chief Inspector Finney, here, thinks you might be able to help. I think Chief Inspector Finney might be right. We need a hint, before this thing gets out of hand . . . so, if you know the words, sing. Now! Because, ten seconds from now, I'm going to walk out of here and, when they ask, I'm going to tell 'em. That Chief Inspector Finney has been with *me* all morning, in the C.I.D. Office. Checking statements. Studying the file. If necessary, we can bring witnesses . . . enough witnesses to make you, or anybody else, the biggest liar this side of Mars.

'So-o . . . whatever happens to you, within the next few minutes, *we* don't know. We're not here. We're three miles away, busy doing our own job.' Holmes paused, stared into Page's face then, very deliberately, added, 'It's a fix, Inky. It'll stick. It may not be in "the book" . . . but we're not talking about "the book". We're talking about information. Grab that. Hang onto it . . . or it'll be something for you to think about, while you're waiting for the stitches to come out.'

Page's breathing rasped at the back of his throat. Just once, he flicked his eyes at Finney, as if in confirmation, and he was convinced.

He spoke to Holmes.

He groaned, 'Scarfe.'

'Come again,' rumbled Finney.

'Scarfe.' Page's voice gained a little strength. 'Frank Scarfe. He took the watches. I dunno about the silver . . . but I wouldn't be surprised.'

'*Alderman* Scarfe?' Disbelief and fury fought each other in Finney's question.

Page nodded.

'You're a bloody liar!' exploded Finney.

'No.' Something not too far removed from triumph touched the words. 'I ain't lying. But, that's something you *don't* wanna know. It ain't worth a thumping any more, is it? But, that's who . . . supposing you ever check. Frank Scarfe. Your big-time father-in-law . . . *Mister*-bloody-Finney.'

Myra Finney still wore her torn nightdress and soiled house-coat. Had her mother been able to see her, she would have railed against the sloppiness of her daughter. But, she couldn't see. She could only hear.

Myra Finney was holding a telephone conversation with her mother.

'How are the kids? They behaving themselves? . . .'

'Well, don't spoil 'em. You spoil 'em, then Ralph gets mad and takes it out on me . . .'

'I know. But that doesn't help much. If you didn't spoil 'em, every time they come to visit, it wouldn't happen, would it? . . .'

'Where is he? . . .'

'Oh—of course—he would be. I wish Ralph could get himself interested in things like that . . .'

'Ralph' had things on his mind. He walked alongside Holmes and scowled at the surface of the tarmac path a few yards ahead of their feet.

He growled, 'That was a nice play, in there, Holmes.'

'Eh?'

'With Page. Threatening to leave me to sort him out. It scared blue shit out of him.'

'Bluff,' said Holmes, flatly.

'Wassat?' Finney turned his head and stared at the detective sergeant.

Holmes said, 'I go so far. No farther.'

'Meaning?'

'Can't you guess?'

'I can make a few guesses,' said Finney, harshly. 'Which would earn me a coconut?'

'One swing . . . and, even that was one too many.'

'You being funny, sergeant?'

'I'm being realistic, chief inspector. If Page lodges a complaint . . .'

'He wouldn't *dare*.'

'Not after my little speech . . . I hope. But, if he does, you have the limb all to yourself.'

'Hold it!' Finney stopped and faced Holmes. He narrowed his eyes, and said, 'You'd drop me?'

Holmes met look with look, moved his lips in a quick, tight smile, then said, 'Chief inspector, if Page *does* complain, you're already bouncing. Nobody airs his muscles on my future.'

'You bastard.'

'Occasionally, by inclination . . . but, never by birth.'

'I thought I could trust you, Holmes.'

'Sure.' Holmes bobbed his head in a nod. 'You can trust me, Chief Inspector Finney. You can trust me *never* to be a mug.'

Finney turned and stomped along the path. Holmes walked alongside him.

Finney growled, 'I'll see you at the car, sergeant.'

He turned at a fork in the path and strode towards the potting shed, and the head gardener.

54

'Yes, all right, mother. Tomorrow night . . .'

'I can't say what time—not for certain—Ralph works all hours. You know how it is . . .'

'Oh, yes. Before their bed-time. We'll get them back here, before late. But I can't give a definite time . . .'

'Right. And give my love to father. Tell him I hope he enjoyed the match . . .'

'Well?' asked the head gardener.

'We can't prove anything,' Finney said.

'Uhu?' The head gardener examined the cold bowl of his cherry-wood.

'We deal in proof. Legal proof. It has to stand up in court—against cross-examination—and, without it, we're help-less.'

'What you're telling me,' said the head gardener, carefully, 'is that thieves get away with things. Right?'

'Often. Too bloody often.'

'Not here, they don't,' said the head gardener, heavily.

'Look, I haven't accused him of . . .'

'You don't have to. Thanks for the hint.'

'He'll deny it, and there isn't a scrap of proof.'

'He'll deny *what*?' The head gardener's look was full of meaning. 'You've just called in to tell me you've finished with Page . . . that's all.'

'That's all,' agreed Finney, flatly.

11 a.m. . . .

The woman scraped the last of the left-overs into the mouth of the garbage-disposal-unit, then stacked the plate and knife into the automatic dish-washer. She closed lids and flicked switches, and the kitchen was filled with soft clatters and gentle babbles. She lifted the receiver from the wall telephone, dialled

55

a number, held her lips close to the mouthpiece and spoke in little more than a whisper.

She replaced the receiver, and felt like . . .

Dammit, she felt much as she'd felt the day she'd had to have Tiger put down. Part-martyr-part-traitor. As then, it was necessary, but the necessity carried an almost unbearable hurt. The old cat, and the old husband . . . or was it the old cat, and the new Timothy?

Either way, life was hell.

There was a pain. A distinct, physical pain somewhere deep inside her body. Heart-ache? That's what the romantics might have called it, but she wasn't a romantic. All this good living —all these kitchen gew-gaws—didn't come from romantic dreaming. Her way of life was the end-product of realism; hard decision-making; knowing how to say 'No', without qualification, and without skating round the edges.

Jesus!

The people who must have (albeit temporarily) hated her. Some of the manuscripts she'd returned, with a curt note attached; the classic, single stab which, in the long run, hurts less than the drawn out agony of a negative guyed up as a possibility. She hadn't hesitated. She'd known that (in effect) she was throwing a person's guts back in their face, but she hadn't hesitated. And, some of them she'd met, and some of them she'd liked, but she'd never jibbed at doing the right thing; at doing what *she* believed was the right thing.

Nor had she made many mistakes.

But, this one . . .

This wasn't make-believe. This was for *real*. This wasn't literature—good, bad or indifferent . . . this was *life*. Her life! And his, and Timothy's. This was too close, too near and too painful.

This time she was going to hurt somebody who really *mattered*.

56

(Something was happening. He didn't know what, but he could guess.

Beyond the closed door of Number Three Interview Room, he could hear the bustle of coming and going. The rise and fall of animated conversation. The hurried footsteps . . . sometimes, even running.

The police station was humming, like a disturbed bee-hive. He could guess why.

Eventually, they'd remember him . . . then, he'd tell them. He'd tell a senior police officer. Nobody else.

Until then, he could wait.)

'Scarfe's?'

Holmes glanced sideways, at Finney's stone-faced profile, as he asked the question.

'Where else?'

'I'd have thought . . .'

'What, sergeant? *What* would you have thought?'

'Another officer. In view of things.'

'You . . . for example?'

'No. A more senior officer.'

'Really?' Finney's tone was rip-saw harsh. There was anger in it. And disgust. But, above all else, there was furious determination. He drove the Merc. as only a crack driver can drive; automatically, and at speed, but with one part of his mind free to concentrate upon things in no way connected with the handling of the car. 'You think the chief constable? Gilliant?'

'For God's sake!'

'Or maybe Sullivan? Or Bear?'

'Look, all I'm saying is . . .'

'Harris? Lennox?' Finney snapped the names off, like rotten twigs; starting at the top and working down, through the two deputy chief constables, the assistant chief constable (crime) and ending with the chief superintendent, Head of C.I.D.

57

Holmes said, 'Lennox wouldn't be a bad idea.'

'That fat ape.'

'He's going to have to know . . . sooner, or later.'

'He'll know, sergeant.'

'Well, then . . .'

'When I've nailed the old sod.'

Holmes waited for Finney to brake at traffic lights, then swing left when they turned to green.

He said, 'He's your father-in-law, Ralph.'

'The rank,' snarled Finney, 'is chief inspector. If you don't like playing with that mouthful, I'll accept "sir".'

'*Sir*,' said Holmes, tightly.

'And I don't give a damn who he is. This policing lark, sergeant. It's a rat-race. If you haven't worked that out already, I'm giving you good advice. Your own grandmother . . . that, or you're no damn good as a copper.'

'Nevertheless . . .'

'There's no such word. It's all, or fuck-all.'

Holmes was silent for a moment, then he said, 'I think you're crucifying yourself.'

Finney growled, 'I think I'm doing my job. Now, *shut up*!'

'Sir,' murmured Holmes.

And, at Harrogate Cricket Ground the cloud cover thickened, the air became sultry and the Yorkshire middle-order batsmen struggled against the inswingers being delivered by the Hampshire bowlers.

Frank Scarfe sat in the Members' Stand, glanced at the greying skies, flapped his hand to discourage the swarms of thunder-bugs disturbed by the recent mowing of the out-field, and wondered where the hell all the Yorkshire cricketers had gone.

Leyland (for example) would have knocked this lot to Jericho, and beyond. This ground . . . good God, compared with Headingley, it was little bigger than a putting-green; a firm defensive on-drive and the boundary was *there*. Close, too, could have shown 'em the way. Or young Hutton.

Where the hell *had* all the meat of Yorkshire cricket gone?

His neighbour said, 'If it rains, and we get a sticky wicket, we're in trouble.'

'We're in trouble, as it is,' complained Scarfe.

'A bad patch,' said his neighbour, philosophically.

Scarfe sniffed, and said, 'Sutcliffe would have still been *there*.'

'Sutcliffe's in a wheel-chair,' said his neighbour, sadly.

Scarfe grumbled, 'He could *still* do better than this lot.'

'We're building up a team.'

'Aye . . . they've been saying *that* for years.'

The man thought . . .
She'll be seeing him, today. She must. Before night. Before
bedtime. She has to see him.

There'll be an excuse. A reason. A lie, but a good lie . . .
and she'll tell it well. She'll tell it well, because she doesn't
want to hurt me.

Isn't that odd? That she doesn't want to hurt me? As if I
still had feelings left to hurt. As if I still had enough dignity
to take offence.

God bless her . . . she will lie.

She walked in, from the kitchen, and he said, 'F-finished, already?'

'All mod cons.' She smiled, as she spoke.

'Y-yes. You've done w-well for yourself.'

'I think so.' Her tone was brisk. A false and deliberate brisk-ness. She glanced at her wrist-watch, then said, 'That—er—that reminds me. I'm sorry—I'll put it off, if you like—but I should be meeting an author, in just over an hour. Half-past twelve. It's not a matter of life, or death, but . . .'

'P-please.' He raised his hand a few inches.

'He'll be disappointed. But, I don't mind disappointing him, for your sake.'

'N-no. Don't disappoint him.'

'If you're sure.' She looked worried.

'Qu-quite sure.' He moved the raised hand in a vague gesture. 'I—er—I think *I'd* better let a few p-people know I'm b-back.'

'The firm?' She looked at once uncomfortable and startled.

'No . . . just p-people.' His lips bent and parted and, for a moment, it looked as if he might laugh, but the moment passed. He said, 'I'm not an ac-accountant any more. Tax laws. This new V.A.T. thing . . . n-new to me. I w-wouldn't know where to start. B-book-keeping. I might be able to do that. N-nothing more involved, these days.'

She touched her mouth with the tips of her fingers, looked at him with a depth of sadness for a moment, then said, 'You never *do* . . . do you? It's only at moments like this. It makes you realise.'

'What?'

'The so-called "debt to society". It's never paid in full.'

'C-compound interest.' It was meant to be a mild joke, but it didn't come off.

'It's cruel,' she said.

'What other way?' he asked.

'There must *be* another way.'

'N-no. He closed the fingers of his right hand, and examined the close-clipped nails. He seemed to speak, musingly, at the bent fingers. 'We can l-land men on the moon. We can even analyse the surface of Mars. Television. Travel faster than sound. Heart-transplants. K-kidney-transplants. Miracles . . . except with our own m-minds. A m-man goes wrong, and the only t-treatment left is to handle him like a wild animal. Lock him away. P-put him behind bars. And th-they haven't yet realised.' Gradually, his voice veered towards bitterness. 'C-cage any other animal, and it becomes different. A different creature. Its balance of normality changes. It becomes wild and unmanageable. That, or it becomes terrified and a pathetic thing. It *changes*. Its nobility—whatever nobility it might possess—is crushed. Either way, it becomes base.

'Man . . . he's an animal. All those men I've left in prison . . . they're all animals. What else? They, too, become base. Of course there must be another way. A *better* way . . . there couldn't be a *worse* way. But, in that line of human achievement, the moon's still made of cheese. Monsters still inhabit Mars. *There*, we still have the little man with his red flag, walking in front of the motor car.' As before, the speech impediment disappeared as the intensity of his words increased. He looked up at her, and said, 'W-we can't change it. N-nuts and bolts. Transistors. Technology. Th-they've had pride of place for t-too long. P-pride of *man* doesn't count any more.'

'Call in at the office,' said the head gardener. 'Pick up your cards. Don't come in Monday.'

'Why?' Page stopped dabbing his swollen lip, and gazed, wide-eyed and disbelieving. 'What have I done wrong?'

'You don't have to have a reason,' said the head gardener, coldly.

'The hell I don't!'

'You're "unsatisfactory". That's reason enough.'

'What have I done wrong?' repeated Page.

'I've just said.'

'It's that bastard Finney, isn't it? It's *him*.'

'Who?'

'The copper. It's summat *he* said.'

'The police asked permission to speak to you. It's right they should.'

'And?'

'They called in, to say they'd finished with you. That's all.'

'I'll bloody bet!'

'Don't call me a liar, Page,' said the head gardener. 'I don't like being called a liar.'

'Well that, mate, is what you are,' said Page, tightly. 'A puffed-up, sanctimonious liar. And, it's time somebody told you.'

'Call for your cards, on your way home.'

'Go to hell. Send 'em. You know my address.'

The head gardener sighed.

'And a month's wage,' added Page. 'One month's notice, or salary in lieu . . . don't forget that part.'

'You'll get it.'

'And listen, mate,' warned Page. 'I still got friends in this job. Any wild talk about why you sacked me—even a hint that isn't truth, full-bore . . . I can still afford a solicitor. Just remember that.'

As he turned to leave the fern-house, the head gardener said, 'You're unsatisfactory. It's reason enough. I don't have to invent reasons.'

Noon . . .

The woman wore a lightweight, belted mac. Knotted to the sling of her shoulder-bag was a brightly-coloured head-scarf as an acknowledgement to the promise of rain.

She said, 'I'll—er—I'll go, then. I'll cut it as short as possible.'

'You look v-very smart,' observed the man, solemnly.

'Career-girlish.'

'No.' A sad, faraway look washed over his eyes for a moment, then he murmured, 'L-lovely. You look v-very lovely.'

The woman thought . . .

I'm not leaving him. I can't leave him. Rape? God help me ...
that's twelve years since. He's been punished. More than
punished. And, without help—my help—his punishment will
be never-ending. It will be almost that, as it is. But, without
me, it will be multiplied and beyond any man's endurance.
All right ... now my punishment starts.
But, I won't leave him.

She made a movement towards her shoulder-bag, and said, 'Do
you want a key? If you're going out ...'

'I—er—I won't be b-back, before you.'

'If you're quite sure.'

'I'm s-sure.'

'Okay.' The act was pure, brisk, housewifely affection ...
if it *was* an act. 'I'll have a meal ready. What time?'

'N-no.' He shook his head, slowly.

'You mean ...'

'I d-don't know what time I'll be back. M-maybe late. I
have some p-people to see.'

'You'll need a meal.'

'I'll—I'll eat out.'

'Sure?' A hint of worry was there, now. Genuine worry.

He nodded.

'Okay.' She stepped nearer, and kissed him on the forehead. Again, the perfect gesture of 'temporary goodbye' from
a loving wife. She turned for the door, and said, 'See you later,
pet.'

The man thought ...
No you won't, darling.
It may, or may not, have been a mistake coming here. This
flying visit—these last few hours of exquisite hell—may, or
may not, have been necessary but, at least, I now know.
What doubts I had ...

What hopes I still clung to ...
They were empty doubts. Empty hopes.
You won't 'see me later', darling. You'll never see me again.

Rooms can have atmosphere. The walls and furniture can bounce back the moods of the occupants—sometimes the mood of a single occupant, if that mood is strong enough and furious enough—and the whole room becomes charged with a subtle, but distinct 'feel'. Thus rooms can contain happiness, as surely and as certainly as a can can contain soup or beans. Or misery. Or hatred. Or even evil ... as any tourist visitor to the long-dead Himmler's private villa will willingly vouchsafe.

Finney's office had an atmosphere.

Part anger, part frustration, part disbelief, part outrage. It built up to a near-physical thing; as if the office itself was a time-bomb, about to explode any second. As if Finney, himself, might explode.

Holmes murmured, 'Easy. It happens, sometimes.'

'Don't tell me to be "easy", sergeant,' stormed Finney. 'The *bastard*! He's been laughing at me, for all these years.'

'If what Page says is true.'

'If?'

'He could be lying. We don't yet know.'

'He wouldn't dare.'

'We don't yet know,' repeated Holmes.

'Sergeant, don't be a bloody fool.'

'All I'm saying is ...'

'An alderman,' rasped Finney. 'My own bloody father-in-law. Page isn't going to risk making a false cough on *that* level. All right ... he enjoyed himself, doing it. But, that's *why*. You know Page. You know how these microbes think. He wouldn't have the guts—he wouldn't have the *nerve*—not unless it was true.'

64

'In which case, I think . . .' began Holmes.

'Don't you bloody-well dare!' exploded Finney. 'Sergeant Holmes, don't you have the blind-born gall to even *suggest* that any other hand but mine feels the hound's collar. That's the one good thing that's come out of it. He's *mine* . . . and, by Christ, I'll cripple any man who even tries to take him away from me.'

'Your father-in-law,' said Holmes, gently.

'That's why.'

'Your wife's father.'

'For God's sake . . . that's *why.*'

'I don't get it.' Holmes shook his head in puzzlement. 'I mean . . . your own flesh and blood. We-ell, more or less.'

Finney flopped into the desk-chair. He rested his arms on the surface of the desk, and stared at his hard-clenched fists.

'Holmes,' he muttered, hoarsely, 'do you love your wife?'

'Yes. Why not?'

'After how many years?'

'Fifteen. Fourteen . . . closing fifteen years.'

'And you still love her?'

'Of course.' Holmes's voice was low with embarrassment. This was a new Finney; a Finney he'd never seen before; a Finney he wasn't too happy with. He said, I don't see . . .'

'It doesn't follow, y'know,' growled Finney.

'Sir?'

'You said "Of course". There's no "of course" about it.'

'No, sir. I—er—I suppose not.'

'Cut out the "sir", Holmes.'

'Back there—in the car—you said . . .'

'I don't give a damn what I said back there in the car. Cut out the "sir". I'm in need of a friend, not a subordinate.'

Holmes moved his shoulders.

'Fifteen years, eh?' He looked up into Holmes's face, and

said, 'With me, it's barely ten years . . . and I hate the sight of the bitch.'

'Sir—er—Ralph . . .' Holmes moved his hands in a helpless, meaningless gesture. 'I don't think you should be telling me these things.'

'Why not?'

'They're—er—well, they're private. You might regret.'

'You think I'm a bastard—a right, ring-tailed bastard—don't you?'

'No. I've never . . .'

'Not just you. Everybody. Every copper who knows me.'

'You're keen,' admitted Holmes, warily.

'I'm a bastard, boy,' Finney grinned a quick, lop-sided grin that contained no humour. 'I take it out on other people, because I can't take it out on her.'

'Look, I don't want to . . .'

'Remember a year back? Just over a year back?'

Holmes nodded.

'I spilled over . . . remember?'

'I remember.'

'I marked her a little. Not much—not as much as she deserved . . . but a little. It's not "gentlemanly". I'm not arguing that it was "gentlemanly". But, it was the only medicine left. She was a slut . . . and, dammit, she's *still* a slut.'

'Ralph, I don't think you should . . .'

'Gilliant gave me hell,' mused Finney. 'He roasted me to the bone. But—y'know—I had this feeling. That his heart wasn't in it. That he was going through the motions, because he'd been *told* to go through the motions. Oh, he was mad. The "reputation of the force" . . . all that bullshit. And, he'd have bust me, without a second's hesitation. I'm not saying it was *all* guff. But it was spread a bit too thick. A lot too thick, for a man like Gilliant.'

'Scarfe?' murmured Holmes.

'Who else? Alderman-bloody-Scarfe. I'd laid violent hands on his beloved daughter . . . and that she'd deserved it didn't matter a spit-in-the-wind damn. I was only a copper. A dogsbody detective chief inspector. But *he* was a flaming alderman, and the big pot of the police authority. I've never been allowed to forget that, sergeant. Never!'

Holmes offered a tentative opinion. A slight argument.

He said, 'Gilliant. I can't think he'd do that . . . let the standing of your father-in-law sway him. He's not the kind.'

'They're *all* the bloody kind,' sneered Finney, bitterly. 'You think he's going to put his job in hock for the likes of me?'

'No, but . . .'

'He roasted me, sergeant. And, I'd to stand there and take it.'

'Rightly, or wrongly, he thought you deserved it.'

'That's what *you* think.'

'Knowing Gilliant,' agreed Holmes.

'You believe in love . . . eh?' sneered Finney.

'I can't see what that has to do with . . .'

'Your wife, sergeant.'

Holmes said, 'Yes. I love my wife,' in a quiet, solemn voice.

'I bloody-well *don't*,' muttered Finney. 'She was a tart when I married her. She's still one . . . and not a particularly clean tart, either.'

'For God's sake, Ralph!'

'But, I'm ambitious . . . see? Always have been. Scarfe's daughter. She could help . . . if not her, her old man. That was the big idea. They're all the same, on their backs. They're all the same with a sack over their heads. I'd sleep with her. I'd push a wedding ring on her finger. I'd give her kids. Anything! A means to an end . . . get it? *My* end. I had my eye on big things. He was Councillor Scarfe, in those days, but he was going places. Even I could see that. So-o, I hitched my wagon to his star, sat back, shagged his daughter and kicked hell out

67

of every penny-farthing crook I could lay my hands on.' Finney paused and, for a moment, Holmes thought the detective chief inspector was actually going to turn his head and spit on the carpet. Instead, he continued, 'I got a name. I'm still proud of that name. *Very* proud. Anybody *I* book always goes down. Always! They go down big. I don't piss around. I throw the book at 'em. I lay it on with a shovel. Okay . . . I've even been known to cook the evidence a little. But the buggers sweat blood when they see *me* go into the witness-box. They know no smart-arsed lawyer's going to shift *my* evidence. They're going down, sergeant. They're going down for a long, long time. They know it. I know it . . . and now, *this*.' For a split second Finney's face seemed to be on the point of crumbling, but he pulled himself together, dragged a deep, shuddering breath into his lungs, and ended, 'A lot of people are going to laugh, sergeant. A lot of people are going to cheer. But, by God, not for long! This one I *will* nail . . .'

'If it's him.'

'It's *him*,' snarled Finney. 'I can feel it, in my guts. And I'll personally melt the bloody key.'

(The fat man waddled into Number Three Interview Room, and closed the door behind him. He was far more than ordinarily 'fat'. He was obese. Arms and legs apart, he was the perfect large sphere, with a smaller sphere balanced atop. That was his figure; a freakish figure garbed in freakish clothes.

He said, 'My name's Lennox. The bloke at the counter said you might still be here.'

'Are you a detective?'

'Aye.' The globular head bobbed.

'A senior detective?'

'Chief superintendent.'

'You'll do.'

'That's handsome of you, old son. What puzzles me is why

you're still here. Three o'clock in the morning, thereabouts. A five-hour wait, so I'm told. Must be important.'

'Very important.'

'Ah, well.' The fat detective lowered himself into the spare chair, and the tubular steel squeaked in gentle protest. 'I suppose we'd better compare notes as to what is, and what isn't, "important". You know my name. What about telling me yours?')

Page watched from the windows of the kiosk, as he waited for the operator to answer his dial. With cops, you never knew. With animals like Finney, you *never* knew. He could be around, in some damn car, somewhere. He could be (what was the cockeyed expression they used?) 'keeping observations'. He could, too. He could be 'keeping observations' at this very minute. Snooping around, playing it smart. With that one, you couldn't trust . . .

The operator's voice cut in on his thoughts.

Page said, 'I—er—I want Harrogate Cricket Ground, please. The number. The number of the Members' Enclosure. There'll be a bar. A refreshment room. Something. That's the number I want, please.'

Myra Finney did her weekend shopping.

She used the supermarket. She pushed the trolley slowly up one lane of piled food, and down another. Slowly. Almost dreamily. She steered the trolley with her left hand, while her right dipped onto the shelves and dropped articles into the deep, wire receptacle.

There was no 'shopping list'. No method. No previously thought-out plan of housewifery. If a packet, or a tin, caught her eye—if the label was gaudy enough to stand out from its fellows—that was enough. The words 'sale' and 'reduction' brought an immediate response. The word 'bargain' was never passed unheeded.

From above her head, strategically placed speakers sprayed the shoppers with musical deodorant; non-music, spun-sugar-sweet and with the volume turned low, on the off chance that its very insipidity might, should it be too intrusive, drive the musically-minded from the premises.

Slowly—like a sleep-walker meandering around an Aladdin's cave of 'instant' food, none of which had to be bought—Myra Finney did her weekend shopping.

At the pay-out, she wrote a cheque. She trundled the trolley out into the car park, opened the boot of the Morris and began to transfer the purchases from trolley to boot. A look of innocent, bovine surprise touched her expression as, for the first time, she realised how much tinned and packet-sealed food she'd bought.

Page said, 'Thanks, I've got that. Eight-one-three-nought-one. And the prefix is nought-four-two-three. Thanks.'

As he mouthed the words he jotted the numbers onto the cover of the tattered directory. He replaced the receiver, searched the street with frightened eyes, then brought a bundle of coins from his pocket and sorted through them.

The man sought a mac. The sky promised rain, and it seemed sensible to be prepared. He went into the master bedroom and slid back one of the doors of the fitted wardrobe.

And, why not?

Why *shouldn't* there be a couple of pairs of men's casuals in among the high-heels, the courts and the sandals? Why *not* a pair of newly-laundered men's pyjamas, on one of the shelves? Why not the dressing-gown? *Or* the lightweight, plastic mac which buttoned left over right? . . . a fine evening was no guarantee it wasn't going to be raining next morning.

One good thing about plastic macs. If they fitted a man of

average build, they also fitted *another* man of average build.

He eased the plastic mac from its hanger, then closed the sliding door.

12.10 p.m. . . .

Page spoke into the mouthpiece of the public telephone; he did little to disguise his voice, because there was nothing about his voice which might make it immediately recognisable. It was a very ordinary voice, but it carried absolute conviction.

He said, 'It doesn't matter who I am. We've done business in the past. That's all you need to know . . . that I know *who* you are, and *what* you are. Somebody's lifting good class silver. I could guess who, but that isn't important, either. You're taking it, Scarfe. No—don't interrupt, I haven't the coins to make this a long call . . . just take it from me, I *know* you're taking it. And Finney knows. Your son-in-law. *He* knows. And, I don't have to tell you what that means. Get rid of it. Shift it. Dump it. Let's call this a favour, from one old friend to another. Let's call it that . . . but, for Christ's sake, *believe* it.'

He pushed the receiver onto its rest, before Scarfe could answer, then pushed open the door of the kiosk and scurried into hiding among the throng of Saturday shoppers.

'He'll be at Harrogate.' Finney had quietened his disgust. He was smoking a cigarette, and his voice was its old harsh, no-nonsense growl. He said, 'Yorkshire's playing Hampshire. That's where he'll be. He never misses a home match. That means there'll be a couple of assistants ticking things over, at the shop. We'll twist *their* tails . . . you never know.'

'We'll be lucky,' observed Holmes.

'There'll be safes. Maybe a spare key.'

'Now, that *would* be foolish.'

'That bastard,' said Finney, 'has been at it for too long.

7<small>1</small>

That's if Page isn't spinning the fanny . . . and I don't think he is. He's been at it for years. People get careless, sergeant. They get cocky. They think they *can't* come unstuck. You never know.'

'Possible.' Holmes still sounded very doubtful.

Finney stood up, and said, 'But, first a meal. There's a Chinese dump, down the road. It puts on a pretty good sweet-and-sour.'

'I don't go for Chinese food,' said Holmes.

'Okay. You have egg, sausage and chips. They cater for the common herd, too. I feel good . . . my treat.'

The woman threaded the Cortina along the narrow passage, alongside *The Green Man*, towards the patrons' car park at the rear. She was a careful driver but, this time, she drove even slower than usual.

'Lovely,' he'd said. 'Very lovely.' And, he'd meant it. He'd *really* meant it. The bad old take-it-for-granted days were a thing of the past. A time of the past; a time with a dividing wall of twelve tortured years separating them from the present.

She parked the car with exaggerated care.

The woman thought . . .
Anywhere. Any other time. Any other person.

But, why has it to be here, now and with Tim? And—in God's name—why has it to be me?

Because I'm still his wife?

I was his wife yesterday. Last week. A month ago. A year ago. Twelve years ago . . . I was his wife, then.

Being his wife is only part of it. A not very important part of it. I've been his wife for the last twelve years. Through the affair with Martin. When I met Tim—when I fell in love with Tim—all the times I've shared my bed with Tim . . . and, before that, with Martin. I've always been his wife.

For Christ's sake!

Why is it suddenly so important?

The weakest excuse I have—no excuse at all . . . but the only excuse I can offer.

('*Meaning you were framed,' rumbled the fat dectective.*

'*No, sir. Not framed.'*

'*That's what you're saying, old son.' Lennox fished around in the shapeless pockets of a shapeless blazer and found a pipe. It was one of those pipes with a carved bowl; the sort of pipe seen tucked away in tobacconists' windows, but rarely seen between the teeth of a pipe-smoker. The bowl was elaborately carved into the resemblance of a bull's head. In size, the pipe looked as if it might hold an ounce of tobacco at one filling, and bring on jaw-ache if it was held in the mouth for a prolonged period. Apropos of nothing in particular. Lennox grinned, and said, 'I used to smoke cigars. Cheroots, actually. But, the cats didn't like 'em.'*

'*Cats?'*

'*The bane of a man's life, old son.'*

'*Oh!'*

'*Worse than women, for sulking. And, when the missus is on their side, they win hands down.'*

'*Look—I'm sorry—but . . .'*

'*And, they didn't go for the cheroots, see? So, I took to this thing.' He eyed the pipe, morosely. 'It ain't the same. Too much packing, and tapping and general mucking about. Now . . . you were talking about being framed.'*

'*No. Not exactly framed . . .'*)

The man walked the pavement and fought to suppress an illogical desire to run. To run away . . . but, from what? Not the crowds. These people weren't a *crowd*. By comparison with the sardine-tin conditions of jail these streets were *deserted*. Footsteps on flagstones were nothing, after years of hearing footsteps on iron grills. Traffic noise was soothing, when placed alongside the babble of the dining hall or the exercise yard.

So, run away from *what*?

Freedom!

The answer to the mental question slammed home, like a rebound.

He was scared of freedom. The thing he'd dreamed about. The thing he'd waited for. The thing which, in his imagination, had kept him sane . . . had kept him *alive*. And, now he had it, it terrified him.

Example . . .

He was on his way to Bank Street. Number twenty-seven, Bank Street. He knew the city; he knew where Bank Street was. The houses had numbers, therefore the finding of number twenty-seven posed no problem.

But, how to get there?

That had been the problem.

To take a taxi? To take a bus? To walk?

There'd been a choice, which meant there'd been a decision. And decision-making was part of *freedom*. He could go to bed when he liked; get up when he liked; eat when he liked; eat *what* he liked; wear what he liked; talk to whom he wished to talk; walk, or ride, wherever he wished to walk, or ride, see goods on display in shop windows and, if a thing caught either his eye or his fancy, buy that thing.

Normality. Freedom. Decision after decision after decision.

For twelve years, he'd obeyed instructions. From the screws, from the block bosses, from the bully-boys. Never refusing—never being allowed to refuse . . . never having to *decide*.

Even this morning . . .

He'd bathed, when she'd told him to bath. He'd put on the clothes she'd told him to put on. He'd eaten a meal—a ridiculously inappropriate meal—because she'd told him he must eat it.

74

But, now . . . nobody. Nobody to *tell* him. To walk, to take a taxi or to take a bus.

This was the dream . . . the golden, sour-centred, terrifying dream.

This was *freedom*!

He shoved his hands deeper into the pockets of the plastic mac, dropped his chin onto his chest, gritted his teeth and forced himself to walk normally, towards Bank Street.

He *forced* himself to be free.

12.30 p.m. . . .

When he wasn't using it to transfer food from the plate to his mouth, Finney used the fork as an addendum to his philosophising. He wagged it above the table, as a means of underlining the words of pseudo-wisdom with which he was boring off the ears of Detective Sergeant Holmes. Like a makeshift baton, with which he conducted his own conversation.

He said, 'Y'know . . . that's why. He's a cunning old sod. Give him that. He's got it all worked out. That's why he refused a seat on the bench. Alderman . . . sure. But, magistrate . . . not on your Nelly. And, why? Because, if some farting little hook came up for nicking, and *he* was on the bench—and if the hook had slipped the loot to *him* . . . I mean, what the hell *then*?'

'Was he offered a seat on the bench?' asked Holmes.

'Sure. A couple of times. He refused.'

'I thought nobody knew these things.'

'About magistrates? All about how they're picked? Don't be innocent, sergeant. They're all vetted. It's supposed to be very hush-hush . . . all the rest of it. They *know*. Who the hell do you think vets 'em? We do . . . who else? Supers and chief inspectors. Damn it all, we don't want Jack the Lad—some berk with a list of convictions as long as your arm—up there

75

dishing out the fines. Now, do we? And, that old sod's been listed twice . . . and refused both times.'

'I didn't know that,' said Holmes, with interest, and through a mouthful of egg and chips.

'Twice. He's been . . .'

'No. I mean that we vetted prospective magistrates.'

'You're not supposed to know. You don't carry the rank . . . that's off the record. But, what I'm saying is this.' Finney waved his fork even more vigorously. 'That's *why*. That's why the cunning old bastard refused. Everything else. He wanted power. He wanted glory. But not *that*. That would have been too dangerous. And all the back-slapping garbage, and the how-are-things-going-Ralph bull. He was always asking about the job. What cases. Who was on the twist. What sort of crimes were we being bothered with. The bloody questions! And me—like a mug—gave him the answers. Why not? My father-in-law. An alderman. Who the hell *can* you trust, if you can't trust somebody like him? But clever . . . eh? He helped me up the ladder. I'm not disputing that. A big-wig in the police authority . . . of course he pulled strings. I'd have made it . . . but, he hurried things along a bit. That's all. And, for why? So he'd have somebody up top, feeding him info. That's what gets me, sergeant. That's what chokes. That I've been taken for a complete ta-ta, all these years. I've been *used*.'

'It would seem,' agreed Holmes, solemnly.

'But, no more.' Finney lowered his fork and began stuffing Chinese food into his mouth. As he chewed, he said, 'Let's get this stuff eaten, and paid for. Then, we'll start. Then—by Christ!—we will *start*.'

Tim Chambers was a man trying desperately to understand, but failing. His world was falling apart, around his ears and, for the life of him, he didn't know why. He shared a secluded corner of the lounge of *The Green Man* with the woman, listened carefully to every word she had to say . . . but, for the life of him, couldn't understand.

He said, 'Look—sweetheart—we have things going for us.'

'We *had*,' she corrected, sadly.

'We still have.'

'Not now.'

'All right, he's your husband.' He hesitated then, in a gentler tone, added, 'He's also an ex-con.'

'You—you haven't seen him.'

'I don't have to see him to know *that*.'

The woman thought . . .
Dear Tim. Dear, sweet, reliable Tim. Conventional, to the last. An 'ex-con'. That sums up everything. Broad arrows. A sack, with the word 'Swag' across his shoulder. If only life was as simple as that! Blacks, whites but no greys. But the world's full of greys, Tim. The whole world is grey.
I wish you were right. I wish it wasn't.
But it is.

She said, 'Tim . . . I'm so unhappy.'

Tim Chambers reached a hand across the table and closed his fingers, protectively, over her clenched fist.

He was a man in love, and saw no reason to hide that simple fact. Approaching the 'good years'; when what little madness he'd ever had in him had been checked and controlled; when experience had taught its lesson, that anger and impatience always did more harm than good. Still with a fit body, which he didn't abuse; still 'young' by the yardstick of this second half of the twentieth century . . . a few years older than her, but still 'young'.

And successful. Electronics was still in its infancy; it would always be in its infancy, because every year the miracle-men came up with a new idea whose corner-stone was electronics.

77

Electronics had taken man to the moon and Mars. Electronics had allied itself with surgery, and saved thousands of lives. Electronics had made world-wide T.V. and radio possible. When the history book of Earth was finally closed, the chapter on electronics would equal, in importance, the chapter on the wheel.

Tim Chambers believed that.

Electronics was one of the most exciting fields of science around. And, although his post, as director of a provincial electronics firm, wasn't too exciting a job, it was *part*. A very safe and secure part. A part which carried a good salary and from where (as it were) he could sit in the comfort of a box, and watch the near-impossible illusions performed on-stage . . . and yet be part of those illusions.

Electronics couldn't go wrong. All the energy industries demanded electronic gear. The communications industries, too. Every firm, of any real size, *had* to have electronics somewhere. Computers, for example . . . industry, finance, even the social services couldn't function without computers. And that meant electronics. Electronics were here to stay, and here to expand beyond any visible horizon.

Which meant he was safe.

No woman could ask for a 'safer' man than Tim Chambers.

And (until now) he'd been a confirmed bachelor.

And that meant just *that*. No horsing around with women, without the snaffle-rein of marriage to keep him on the straight-and-narrow. Not that sort of 'bachelor'. Nor was he either 'gay' or impotent. The 'queers'; he didn't understand them, but nor did he condemn them; he knew a handful—openly, almost proudly, homosexual—and he liked them, and enjoyed their exaggerated conversation, but he wasn't *of* them. They were good company . . . the word 'gay' fitted them perfectly. But, he'd never even been tempted.

As for impotence. Dammit . . . *she* should know. She wasn't the first. She knew that, too; once the thing had gone beyond mild flirtation, he'd made no pretence. But, she wasn't the last of a long queue. There'd been very few. *Very* few.

There'd been months—sometimes years—without a woman. It hadn't been a hardship . . . merely a discipline. A deliberately, self-imposed discipline. Always, there'd had to be that spark; that mysterious you-and-me which fused into 'us'. And, the truth was, that didn't often happen. The quick, roll-in-the-hay thing . . . *that* wasn't it. That was one small rung higher than animals, and he wanted no part of it. And, never had. Nor had he ever paid; the whores—the professional fornicators—were the pariahs of their sex . . . he'd never even looked at *them*.

And now, this.

And now, her.

And now . . . *him*!

He murmured, 'I could make you very happy.'

'I know.' She choked, and her eyes glistened moisture. 'I—I know you could.'

'*He* couldn't. He never did.'

'Tim,' she pleaded. 'He's—he's different. And . . . I'm still his wife.'

Scarfe braked the Jag alongside the first telephone kiosk he encountered.

He climbed from the car, dialled a Leeds number, then fed coins into the slot.

He didn't waste a word.

He said, 'Conboy, you know who this is. I want something getting ready, as soon as possible. Mob-handed, and ready to move when I give the "off". People we can trust. People who can drive. And, people ready to go all the way, if necessary. Keep my name out of it—I don't have to tell you that . . . just get them on the start-line, ready for the word.'

79

He left the kiosk, re-entered the Jag and drove slowly towards the road leading from Harrogate to Bordfield.

Myra Finney had a boiled egg for her mid-day meal.

All the food she'd bought at the supermarket; the scores of tins and dozens of packets at her disposal. in the fridge and on the shelves of the kitchen . . . and, she had a boiled egg.

An egg. Nature's own 'canned food'. Bung it into boiling water, then forget it. If, like Myra Finney, you aren't bothered about its final consistency—whether it's as hard as a brick, or as sloppy as thin gruel—intricacies like 'timing' don't come into the scheme of things. It's easier than opening a tin of spaghetti; you don't even need a can-opener. If you can boil water, that's it . . . you can boil an egg.

You can actually 'prepare a meal', while you're shuffling around from room to room, shifting dust from point 'A' to point 'B' . . . kidding yourself you're 'doing the housework'. You can flop onto the sofa, open one of the 'with it' women's mags, and read all about how to make yourself sexy for the man in your life. You can gawp at the double-page centre-spread of a male nude; wonder why the hell *your* male has slabs of fat where this male has muscles. Daydream about— we-ell, y'know . . . women have feelings too. Remember last night, and how the big slob rolled with his back to you and grunted, 'Christ! Not *again.*' . . . because (according to the experts who write these articles) men aren't supposed to *do* that. Figure he's getting useless in his old age. And—y'know . . . *remember.*

It's nice to remember. Exciting. It gives the old ego a real lift. Because, you could still do it. Given the right surroundings —given the right bloke—and you could *still* drive him out of his mind. Like riding a bicycle . . . you never forget.

And, all this time, you're 'preparing a meal' . . . just as long as that meal's an egg.

Myra Finney had a boiled egg for her mid-day meal.
A very *hard* boiled egg.

('*I think you're leading up to something very special,*' said
Lennox.
'*I'm giving the background, first. The reasons.*'
'*Agree. But, when it comes, it'll be special.*'
'*Yes.*' He nodded sombre-faced agreement.
'*So-o, on paper? That okay with you, old son?*'
'*Is it necessary?*'
'*It's wise. I can't force you . . . but, it's wise.*'
He frowned and said, '*Why do I trust you?*'
'*Why come here, in the first place?*' countered Lennox.
'*You don't look like a policeman.*'
Lennox grinned, and said, '*I've been told that a few times.*'
'*Perhaps that's why I trust you.*'
'*By, and large,*' observed Lennox, '*we're a trustworthy lot.*'
'He *wasn't.*'
'*No.*' Lennox eyed the bull's head bowl of his pipe. What-
ever was smouldering in that bowl was stinking Number Three
Interview Room to high heaven. It smelled remarkably like
fumigating mixture. The fat man raised his eyes, and said,
'*That's why I think we should have it down on paper.*'
'*If you think so.*'
'*Right. I'll see if I can root out a shorthand expert.*'
Lennox made as if to push himself upright.
'*No!*'
'*What?*' Lennox relaxed onto the seat of the chair. '*What
now?*'
'*Nobody else. I don't want a third party.*'
'*Witnesses, old son,*' rumbled the fat detective. '*The law
likes 'em. It* demands '*em.*'
'*Please.*' There was haunting terror in the eyes, as he looked

into Lennox's face. 'I—I think I'd dry up. Just you and me ... please.'

Lennox said, 'I can't do shorthand.'

'I'd dry up. I'd freeze.'

Lennox pursed his rosebud mouth in thought, then said, 'Okay. What about a dictaphone?'

'Just you, and me?'

'And a dictaphone.'

'Right.' He moved his head in a tiny nod then, as an after-thought, he added, 'I won't retract anything, if that's what's worrying you.'

'Sonny.' Lennox frowned then changed his expression into one of fatherly concern. 'Look—we can do this thing, that way ... if that's what you want. I'll borrow a tape-recording gadget, from the Typing Pool, and you just talk. But, eventually, it has to go down on paper ... and you have to sign it. Think about that, son.'

'You think I haven't thought about it?'

'There's nobody twisting your arm ... okay?'

'I know.'

'There's nobody making any fancy promises.'

'I realise that.'

'You came under your own steam. Nobody asked. Nobody sent for you. You haven't been arrested. Nobody's worked a con-trick on you. Nothing!'

'I know all that.'

'At this moment, you're free to walk out of this room—out of this nick—and nobody'll make a move to stop you.'

'I know that, too. You're not telling me anything I don't know.'

'But . . .' Lennox leaned forward, as far as his stomach would allow, and poked the words across with the stem of his pipe. 'I have this feeling, old cock. We're getting towards the trees . . . and we'll soon be in among the tall timber. And, *when we get* there, *you might try some back-pedalling.'*

'I'll not retract a word . . .'

*'Lemme finish,' grunted Lennox. 'What you've said, so far.
You must have gumption enough to know it's going to chase
a few rabbits out of their holes. You've started an enquiry.
Only you know where it might end. But—so far—you're in the
clear. You're the injured party.' Lennox paused, then said,
'It's what might come next that worries me.'*

*There was a silence. Lennox waited for a reaction, but there
was no reply.*

*'All right,' sighed Lennox, 'we'll do things your way. Tape-
recorder, and you can start from the beginning—then go on
from there . . . agreed?'*

'Agreed.'

*'On the strict understanding. If you've bent the rules, what-
ever comes out isn't some sorta off-beat joke. You can stop, any
time you like. If I ask any questions, that doesn't mean you
have to answer 'em. And, if you feel you should have a
solicitor in here with us, just ask . . . he'll be sent for.' Lennox
stared hard across the table. 'That's it, son. My limitations,
and your rights. Is everything clear?'*

'Very clear indeed . . . and, thank you.'

'So?' asked Lennox.

'Set up the tape-recorder.')

Bank Street . . .

It had changed. It had changed, considerably. A dozen
years ago it had been a row of terrace-type houses, gradually
dirtying and decaying themselves into 'slum property'. At that
time, it hadn't yet reached the end of the slide, but it was
gathering speed.

Somebody had rammed on the brakes.

They were still terrace-type houses but, now, *nice* terrace-
type houses. A facing of cement and colour-wash had trans-

formed the walls. New paint, a few window-boxes and twin flower-tubs at some of the doors had done the rest. There was now a quiet 'class' about the street; like a drunk who'd pulled himself together, cleaned himself up and discovered a new-found dignity. There wasn't wealth—nobody with money to spare lived in Bank Street—but there was decency and cleanliness.

As the man turned into Bank Street, his spirits rose a little. Bank Street was concrete proof that the world could some-times change for the better.

A woman answered his tap on the door of number twenty-seven. She was a thin woman; pared down to bare essentials by the sort of life he could readily imagine. Dark hair streaked liberally with grey. Face high-cheek-boned, narrow-nosed and thin-lipped. The eyes were dark; they carried a look of kind-ness, behind a veneer of suspicion.

She said, 'Yes?'

'Mrs. P-Page?'

She nodded.

'Is Mr. P-Page at home, p-please?'

'Who wants to know?'

'You w-wouldn't know me.'

'Does *he* know you?'

He nodded.

'What name shall I tell him?'

The man gave his name.

The eyes narrowed, fractionally, and she said, 'You'd better wait.'

A few minutes later the woman led the man into the house, through the front room and into the tiny kitchen at the rear. Page was sitting at a Formica-topped, drop-leaf table, half-way through a meal of steak and kidney pudding. As each forkful reached his mouth he guided it carefully past a swollen lip.

The two men nodded a silent greeting to each other.

'I'm staying,' warned the woman.

'Of c-course.'

'There's no need . . .' began Page.

'I'm staying,' repeated the woman, firmly.

Page shrugged his shoulders, resignedly.

The woman said, 'Now you're in, you can sit down.' She waved a hand towards a leather-topped kitchen stool. 'But, you're not staying long. And, you're not talking *him* into anything.'

Page chewed at his food.

The man lowered himself onto the stool.

Page swallowed, then said, 'Chambers?'

The man nodded.

'She's still seeing him. Regularly.'

'Who's "Chambers"?' demanded the woman, suspiciously. 'And, who's "she"?'

'His wife.'

'Look! What's happening? What's been going . . .'

'M-Mrs. Page.' The man interrupted the woman's rising anger. 'H-Harry was a f-friend. A g-good friend.'

'In *that* place?' Her thin lips curled.

'F-for the first two years, I n-needed a friend. Th-then he left.'

'He'd done his time. He's been straight, ever since.'

'I d-don't doubt that. He's a g-good man.'

'Don't soft-soap me. Say why you're here . . . then get out.'

Page sighed, and said, 'Ease off, luv. This isn't a proposition. I made him a promise, before I left . . . that's all.'

'What sort of a promise?'

'To keep an eye on his wife.'

'*To keep an eye on his . . .*'

'Not *that,* for God's sake,' said Page, irritably. 'To watch her . . . that's all. To see what she was up to.'

'Snooping?'

'Aye . . . if you like.'

'Of all the . . .'

'Mrs. P-Page,' interrupted the man. 'S-snooping, if you like. I suppose you could c-call it that. But, w-what's the longest you and Harry have been apart? S-separated?'

'Three years.' Her voice was grim and uncompromising. 'That was last time—three years . . . and there isn't going to be a "next time".'

'T-twelve years,' said the man, gently.

'What about twelve years?'

'N-no woman could wait twelve years.'

'*I* could.'

'You haven't been t-tested, Mrs. P-Page.'

'I could still wait. I'm not *going* to, because it isn't going to happen . . . but I could still wait.'

'M-My wife couldn't. Hasn't.'

'And, is that why you're here?'

'That's why he's here,' said Page. He placed his knife and fork across his plate, and continued, 'Now, put a sock in it, luv. I haven't done owt wrong. Just a favour, for a friend . . . that's all. Kept my eyes open, and seen what he *couldn't* see.'

'Snooping,' she muttered, but relapsed into disgusted silence.

Page turned to the man, and said, 'This Tim Chambers bloke. They're thick. Very thick. I get around—parks, gardens, hanging-baskets, that sort of thing . . . and I've seen 'em together often enough. His car parked outside the house, first thing in a morning. That, too. I reckon they're very thick.'

'You've seen th-them with each other?'

'Many a time.'

The man frowned, and said, 'L-love . . . w-would you c-call it s-something important? N-not just in-infatuation.'

'I know what *I'd* call it,' muttered the woman.

'Aye.' Page nodded, slowly. 'More than that. More than infatuation. Like a couple of kids, sometimes. I've seen 'em.

In the park. Running across the grass . . . hand-in-hand. I reckon it's more than infatuation. I'm sorry. But, you *did* ask.'

The woman could contain her outrage no longer.

'Dirty bitch,' she snapped. 'That's what *I* think. And him. Both of 'em. That's what's up with everybody, these days. Sex-mad. Those vows . . . they *mean* summat. They *should*. But, these days they don't. Your husband goes inside—*my* husband's been inside—but that's no excuse. You're mucky if it makes any difference. You've a mucky mind . . . and, that's all there is to it.'

'Hey, luv!' protested Page.

'That's all there is to it,' she repeated, harshly.

The man thought . . .

You're so right, Mrs. Page. By your yardstick, you're so right. Shaw had an expression for it. Mr. Doolittle, and his 'middle-class morality'. Shaw poked Irish fun at it . . . but that was Shaw. Shaw poked fun at so many things that aren't really funny. Things that you count as so right, and so decent. So fundamental.

Why isn't the world like you, Mrs. Page? What's so wonderful about permissiveness? She'd have waited . . . had she been like you, she'd have waited. Twelve years—twenty years— she'd still have waited.

But, she isn't like you.

She isn't better. She isn't worse. She's just different . . . and not so different, at that. Not even different morals. The same morals, grafted onto a different upbringing . . . that's all.

You're so right, Mrs. Page.

And she's right.

You're both right. I'm the one who was wrong . . . twelve years ago. And now, I'm the fly in the ointment. I'm the wasp in the honey-pot. I'm the one who's wrong . . . the thing which shouldn't be here.

'F-Finney?' asked the man. His voice was dead. Cold. Expressionless.

Page touched his swollen lip, and growled, 'As big a bastard as ever.'

'Don't bring Finney into this.' The woman sounded concerned. 'We've had enough trouble. Keep Finney out of things.'

Page ignored his wife's words, and said, 'He's gone places.'

'Twelve years. It's to be ex-expected.'

'Detective chief inspector.'

'As f-far as that?' The man sounded surprised.

Page said, 'He married the Scarfe bint,' and made that sound explanation enough.

'I'd heard the r-rumour. I d-didn't know whether to b-believe it.'

The woman sneered, 'Like gets like . . . and deserves it.'

'Scarfe's an alderman, these days,' growled Page.

The man didn't answer.

'He doesn't deserve to be. He deserves to be behind bars.'

'*And* Finney,' added the woman.

'Finney,' said the man softly. Musingly.

'Don't tangle with him,' advised Page. 'He's mustard . . . worse than he ever was.'

'Ch-chief inspector.'

'Leave him. He'll come unstuck. He'll go too far . . . maybe he has, already. Don't give him the chance to drag you with him.'

The man said, 'W-where's he living, these days?'

'No! Leave him,' warned Page, urgently.

'T-tell me where he's living,' said the man. 'If you d-don't, I'll get to know elsewhere. I'll *g-get* to know.'

The woman looked scared, and said, 'Leave Harry out of this.'

'Harry's n-not in it. N-nobody's in it.'

88

'Raymon Crescent,' said Page, gruffly. 'It's on the outskirts.'

'I know w-where.'

'A house. "White Gates." Fourth—maybe fifth—on the left.'

The man nodded.

'Leave Harry out of it . . . *please*.'

The woman sounded almost desperate. She was a strong-willed woman, married to a weak-willed man; her strength was the strength of them both. And (as she knew, from past experience) the very fringes of lawlessness carried penalties . . . and her man had been smacked around, on this very day, and just *might* be angry enough, and crazy enough, to do the wrong thing.

The man turned to her. He looked into her face and, via words and expression, sought to quieten her fears. He tried to spark the gap between them with his honesty.

He said, 'Mrs. P-Page. I d-don't do my friends a b-bad turn. Harry was g-good to me. About th-the only one. I'm here because he's the only m-man who can tell me th-things I need to know. I d-don't want him with me. I w-walked here. N-nobody saw me. N-nobody will see me leave. That's a p-promise. I've never b-been here. Th-that's a promise, too. I'm not a c-criminal. I c-came out of prison, yesterday . . . b-but I'm not a *criminal*. I want to ask him one more qu-question. That's all. Then, I'll go. You'll never see me again. Either of you.'

There was a silence. The man and the woman stared into each other's eyes. The woman's breast rose and fell as she took deep breaths, before speaking.

She said, 'Harry likes a mug of tea, after his meal. I'll get the mugs from the front room. You can have one with him.'

She left the kitchen.

'Well?' asked Page.

'I n-need a gun.' The man's voice was little more than a whisper.

89

'For Christ's sake . . .'

'Where can I get one?'

'How the hell do I . . .'

'Harry!' For the first time real emotion rode the man's voice. Anger. Desperation. Loathing. They were all there, then they died as he continued, 'I'm not asking you to give me a gun. Or even sell me a gun. I'm asking you *where*. Who *might*. A clue. A pointer. You know more about these things than I do. You can . . .'

'I don't know the boys any more. And, I'm damned if I know . . .'

'Harry . . . I'd prefer a gun to a knife.'

'Oh, my God!'

'That's the only reason. If not one, it's going to be the other.'

'Look—you can't . . .'

'I can walk out of here—into the first sports shop—and buy a knife big enough to do what I'm going to do. But, I'd prefer a gun.'

'Oh, my Christ!' breathed Page. There was the sound of the woman returning. Page leaned forward, and whispered, 'Remember Conboy?'

'The block boss.'

'Word has it he's back in business. In Leeds. That's all I know.'

'Where can I . . .'

'Ask around the boozers. In the centre. That's all I *know*.'

The man smiled his ghost-smile of gratitude.

The woman re-entered the tiny kitchen and placed two mugs on the Formica top of the table.

1.00 p.m. . . .

The Green Man was one of those Edwardian hotels which are proud of their determination not to 'move with the times'.

Its décor (the management would have shuddered with horror, had the expression 'colour scheme' been used) was built around deep reds, dark oak and high chandeliers. The chairs of its lounge were brocade-piped and built to last forever. The tables were spaced far enough apart to ensure complete privacy. The carpet was a custom-made job; thick-piled and with the rich, deep hue of ancient ledgers.

If circumstances demanded sadness, the surroundings provided by the lounge of *The Green Man* gave substance and sympathy to that state of mind.

The woman's fingers were half-closed around the glass of gin and lime on the table. She hadn't yet tasted the drink. She hadn't spoken for at least five minutes. Her misery was a dumb misery; a misery of indecision. It was a very private misery, which Tim Chambers yearned to either share, or dispel.

'Do you love him?' he asked, gently.

She raised her eyes, and said, 'I don't know. Probably.'

'Only "probably"?'

'I'm his wife.'

Chambers hesitated a moment, then said, 'That's not *quite* the same thing, darling.'

She chewed at her lower lip.

'Is it?' he insisted, mildly.

'If only I knew . . .'

They both knew the words weren't an answer to his question, and Chambers waited.

She moistened her lips, and muttered, 'If only I knew where sympathy ended, and love started. If only I *knew*.'

'Ah!' he murmured softly.

'There's a—there's a meeting point.' Her gaze was fixed onto the past; drawing nostalgia into the present in a desperate attempt to grasp something with which she could cope. 'Sympathy. Love. Feeling sorry for somebody. Feeling affection for somebody. There's a blurred area between the two.'

91

'No, there isn't,' he contradicted. 'They're different emotions.'

'That's where I am . . . somewhere in the grey area. And, I don't know which way I'm travelling. I'm lost.'

'Love,' he insisted. 'It isn't sympathy. It isn't just feeling sorry. It's more than that. It's *love*.'

The woman thought . . .

You're only part-right, Tim. Part-right, but part-wrong. Sympathy pre-supposes love. Love includes sympathy, when sympathy's called for. You can't have love without sympathy. You can't have sympathy without love. At this moment, you feel sorry for me because you love me. At this moment, I feel sorry for him.

Sympathy . . . or is it pity? And, if it's pity, where does pity come in this scale of feelings which ends up at love? Pity . . . is it far from the top? Or is it an off-shoot of sympathy and, therefore, a part of love?

And there's another thing . . .

There's twelve years. He's been locked away, for twelve years. And, twelve years isn't a short time. It's a small lifetime . . . to him a complete lifetime. And, even if I hated him twelve years ago—and I did hate him twelve years ago—hatred doesn't last twelve years. Hatred isn't a passive thing. It has to be kept stoked. If it's left alone it shrivels and dies. And what remains is what was there in the first place.

Love?

Do I love him? Did I ever love him? Like you, dear, sweet-tempered Tim? Did I ever love him, as much as I love you?

I don't know. If I knew, that would be the answer.

But, I can't remember—I CAN'T REMEMBER . . . I CAN'T REMEMBER . . .

She stood up from the table and whispered, 'I'm leaving you Tim, darling.'

'You're . . .'

'For now. Until I've sorted this thing out. I've—I've—I don't *know*. If I know—if I ever know—I'll tell you. But he has to be brought into this thing. He has to be given the chance to—to . . .'

She turned and walked from the lounge.

Tim Chambers stared at the untouched gin and lime.

He ran his fingers through his hair, and breathed, 'Why? Why the hell didn't you *die* in prison?'

(*The Grundig tape-recorder made no noise at all. It silently fed tape from spool to spool; recording the words being spoken into the microphone. The microphone sat on the table top; held steady by its circular, lead base. The microphone was positioned about a foot from, and slightly to one side of, the man's face as he talked.*

'*. . . and there seemed nothing wrong. She didn't look sixteen. There must be photographs, somewhere. School photographs. Showing her. And, other photographs. Showing her out of school uniform. Showing her in those shorts she wore. Before they were ripped. I don't know, but I think there must be. Showing the shorts, and the shirt. Before they were ripped. She's the sort. I'm sure she had her photograph taken wearing those things. She was so . . . proud. So sure of herself. I'm sure there must be photographs, showing her. She was that sort of person. Wearing those shorts, that shirt, she looks a lot older than sixteen. She looked years older. She looked at least twenty. More than twenty . . .*')

The man walked into the bank, and presented a cheque for a hundred pounds, across the counter, to the teller. The cheque was made out for cash.

The teller hesitated, then motioned to the head cashier.

The head cashier joined the teller, examined the cheque, then looked through the bandit-glass at the man's face. Recognition came slowly, then the head cashier handed the cheque back to the teller, and said, 'That's quite in order, miss. This customer has been away. He hasn't used the bank for a few years.'

'F-fives, please,' said the man.

The teller counted out twenty five-pound notes. She checked them, then slid them under the glass, towards the man.

The man said, 'I have a d-deposit account.'

'Yes, sir.'

'My wife, too. Sh-she has a deposit account.'

'Yes, sir?'

'I'd—I'd like the money in my deposit account to be t-transferred to my wife's d-deposit account.'

'Certainly, sir. If you just wait, I'll get the forms for you to fill in and sign.'

'The boss isn't around,' observed Finney.

'No, sir. He's at . . .'

'Harrogate. I know. Yorkshire's playing at home. That's where he'll be. Right?'

'Yes, sir. He's a real cricket enthusiast.'

'Lemme see—you're Charterhouse . . . right?'

'Yes, sir.' Charterhouse allowed an obsequious smile to paint itself across his mouth.

Holmes stood at the door of the jeweller's shop, and wondered how Finney would play things.

Finney said, 'You'll be in charge . . . right?'

'Pending Mr. Scarfe's return.'

'Mmm.' Finney rubbed the side of his jaw, strolled the length of the shop, and murmured, 'We have a problem, Charterhouse.'

'Yes, sir?' Charterhouse raised politely interested eyebrows.

94

'We think this place is going to be done.'

'Done?'

'Naughty men, who steal things.'

'Oh!' Charterhouse caught his breath. 'Oh, dear.'

'Nothing definite,' lied Finney, airily. 'Just a hint, that's all. A tip-off.'

Beyond Charterhouse the second assistant looked scared. He was a acne-faced youth, and he'd read of people being injured (even *killed*) when the villains turned their attentions to jewellery emporiums.

'What—er—what should we do?' asked Charterhouse. 'Notify Mr. Scarfe, I suppose.'

'Oh, no—no . . . there's no need for that.' Finney waved a hand. 'If they come—they might not come, but if they *do* come—don't put up resistance. That's all. Let 'em have whatever they want.'

'Yes, but . . .'

Holmes chipped in, 'There's no suggestion it's likely to happen today.'

'Oh!'

'Just a tip-off . . . that's all,' amplified Finney.

'Will we—er . . .' Charterhouse looked, and sounded, vaguely uncomfortable.

'What?' asked Finney.

'Police protection? That sort of thing?'

'Lord, no. We haven't enough concrete evidence to justify that.'

'Rumour,' murmured Holmes. 'That's all.'

'We're here,' said Finney, 'to pass the word. That's all. And to check, of course.'

'Check?' Charterhouse looked puzzled.

'Security . . . the usual thing.'

'Oh . . . I see.'

'The strong-room. It's in the back here . . . right?' Finney strolled towards the rear of the shop. Holmes left his place by the door, and followed.

'Yes. That's right,' said Charterhouse.

'And all the really good stuff's in there?'

'Of course.'

Almost off-handedly, Finney said, 'We'd better have a decko inside. Give the alarm systems a quick once-over. You'll have a key, of course.'

'Oh, yes.'

Charterhouse hurried forward, edged ahead of the detective chief inspector, opened an oak-panelled door and revealed the steel door of the strong-room immediately beyond. He took a key-ring from his pocket, unlocked the door and stood aside.

As Finney opened the door and walked into the strong-room the light inside the windowless room flicked on.

The walls were lined with shelves and, on the shelves were the real treasures of the shop. Each in its own leather-bound case, or under its own glass-topped cover. Rings, pendants, necklaces. Platters, expensive silverware, gold and silver cups. It was a well-stocked strong-room . . . and everything was of above-average value.

Finney nodded towards the safe, in a corner of the strong-room.

'The *real* stuff,' he observed, with mock innocence.

'Precious stones, and metals, sir,' said Charterhouse. 'As you know, we arrange for pieces to be made up to a customer's specification.'

'Uhu.'

'As you probably know, Mr. Scarfe sometimes attends sales. Auctions. Some of these out-of-the-way houses, where they're selling up. He picks up pieces.'

'Picks up?' Finney raised a quizzical eyebrow.

Charterhouse smiled, and said, 'A turn of phrase. He buys them cheap. Ugly pieces, the dealers won't handle. Sometimes broken pieces. He has an eye for a bargain.'

'That I believe,' said Finney, solemnly.

'And we have our own small smelting plant, in the basement.'

'Really?'

'All above-board, of course, sir.'

'An *alderman*? To think otherwise would be tantamount to treason.'

'Er . . . yes, sir,' Charterhouse couldn't decide whether, or not, Finney had cracked an obscure joke.

'We'll check the safe . . . eh?' said Finney, sweetly.

'I'm sorry. I haven't a key.'

'Come on, Charterhouse, don't be cosy.'

'Cosy?'

'Coy. Backward in coming forward. We'll check the safe.'

'Unless *you* have a key,' said Charterhouse, awkwardly.

Holmes said, 'Scarfe—Alderman Scarfe . . . he has a key?'

'Oh yes, sir. Of course.'

'The only key?'

'As far as I know, sir.'

'It figures,' grunted Finney.

'When will he be back?' asked Holmes.

'Monday. He'll call in, before he goes on to the match.'

'Not today?'

'No, sir. We'll be closed, before stumps are drawn.'

'A real cricket buff.' Finney sighed deeply, then said, 'Being his son-in-law helps.'

'Sir?'

'He'll open up, for me . . . as a personal favour. *Before* Monday.'

'Er—I—er...'

'Very interesting.' Finney moved towards the door of the strong-room. Holmes followed him. 'Thanks for showing us round.'

'The—er—the tip-off,' stammered Charterhouse. 'When do you think they . . .'

'Oh, they won't. Finney grinned. 'We'll have a word with 'em. As a special favour. To cross this place off their list. Let's go, sergeant . . . we have work to do.'

From the table alongside the upstairs window of the very 'genteel' café Scarfe had watched Finney and Holmes enter his shop. He now saw them leave and climb into Finney's Merc.

Finney (as Scarfe knew) was very proud of that Merc. It was his own car; a mileage-allowance vehicle, as far as the force was concerned. It wasn't gummed up to hell with radio gadgetry; receivers, hand-mikes, transmitters. It was a very expensive motor car, and Finney wasn't going to let the boffins drill holes in it, and load the boot with wireless junk.

Which was extremely handy . . . from Scarfe's point of view.

Scarfe decided he'd better have another word with his mysterious friend, Conboy.

Myra Finney wondered whether all marriages fell apart. *All* marriages. Not according to the women's mags, of course. Not (that is) until you get to the back and read the letters published in the 'problem page' . . . *then* it made you wonder.

She could have written a letter.

Boy, could *she* have written a letter!

About a husband who, for the first year, or so, couldn't keep his fly zipped . . . but, after that, faded. Not because he was old. Damn it, thirty-five wasn't old. Thirty-five was prime. Thirty-five (according to the experts) was *the* age; post-fumbling and a long time to go before a man was beyond being worked into a lather.

Jesus, what the hell was wrong with him, these days?

It wasn't her. How the hell could it be *her*? She was no

boiler; no mutton-dressed-as-lamb. She was twenty-eight.
Twenty-eight, for Christ's sake, and with a figure to prove it.
Twenty-eight and thirty-five . . . that should be making sweet
music, every night of the week. Just right. The perfect
combination.

Except that it *wasn't*.

It was fifty-million miles from perfection.

Oh, Jesus . . . *why?*

She ran her fingers through her unkempt hair, then bent the
fingers to scratch at a midge bite on the side of her neck. Her
face creased into miserable concentration.

Some other woman?

Okay, let's face it . . . some other woman. It was *one*
answer.

He was no stallion. When he'd married her she'd known
that; that he wasn't the best man she'd ever tasted. He'd been
okay—average—and what he hadn't known she'd tried to
teach him. She'd worked bloody hard that first year. And,
okay—he'd done his best . . . for that first year he'd damn
near killed himself. Willingly. Eagerly. All she'd had to do
was wriggle her backside a little, and he'd been there on the
start-blocks.

But, even in those days, he hadn't been a two-woman man.
At times he'd had to kipper himself to keep *her* happy.

So-o . . .

Maybe that was it. Maybe *that* was why. Maybe some other
hot-arsed little cow was enjoying something that rightly
belonged to *her*. It was *one* answer. Those letters showed it
happened . . . often.

But, by God, if that *was* the reason.

She dropped her hands to her sides, clenched her fists, and
muttered, 'I'll slit her. So help me . . . I'll slit her wide open.'

Then she dropped into an armchair, and her face crumpled,
and she wept her frustrated misery to an empty room.

'On the canal bank.' Scarfe talked into the telephone mouthpiece in a very normal voice. No tremor; no breathlessness; no attempt at disguise. He might have been ordering the groceries, but he wasn't. He was ordering the murder of his son-in-law. He said, 'Ten o'clock, tonight. He'll be there. I'll see to that. There's some old allotments, about a quarter of a mile south of Brent Bridge. There. Ten o'clock, precisely. That's when the police have a shift-change. Not too many uniforms crowding the streets. It'll be just about dark . . . just about right. Send enough men. Hand-picked. No slip-ups. The next time I see him, I want him to be in a morgue.'

He replaced the receiver, fished change from his pocket, then dialled the home number of the man whose death he'd just arranged.

('. . . and then this motor patrol car arrived at the lay-by.'
'Hold it there a minute, son.'
The spools of the tape-recorder continued to rotate.

Lennox had sat, silently; fingers linked across his bay-window gut; head dropped onto his chest and multiplying the folds under his chin. Like a half-dozing Buddha. He raised his head and widened his eyes, as he interrupted.

He growled, 'Don't get me wrong, sonny. Say what you like. Tell me to take a running jump. That's your prerogative. But—as I see things—we're getting to a part that might help. That might help you. It might be wise to make sure you don't miss much. Nobody's likely to be shocked. And, if you're thinking of anybody else's feelings—why start this hare in the first place . . . does that make sense?'

'Yes. It makes sense.'

'Okay, son.' Lennox dropped his head onto his chest, again. 'It's all yours.'

'*The patrol car pulled up, behind us, in the lay-by. It was dark. I didn't know it was a police car. It had its lights on, then they were switched off, when it stopped. I think she knew . . . that it was a police car. I've thought about it a lot. I'm sure she knew. Guessed. It might have had its blue light flashing. Before it stopped, I mean. I don't know how. But, I'm sure she knew.*

'*We'd—er . . . finished. Y'know . . . finished.*

'*She still had her shorts around one ankle. She hadn't taken them off. Not completely. They were hanging to one of her ankles. The left ankle . . . I think it was her left ankle. She'd nothing on, underneath. Just the shorts and the shirt. And the shirt was unbuttoned. She was quite naked, really . . . and we'd just finished.*

'*I had my trousers down . . . about to the knees. And my underpants.*

'*Then—when this police car pulled in, behind us—she started to scream. There was no reason for her to scream. It wasn't as if . . . There was no* reason. *It scared me. Because she'd—she'd enjoyed it. Truly. She'd enjoyed it. So, why should she scream?*

'*Then she scratched at my face. She went wild. She tried to tear her shirt. Then her shorts. She tried to tear them. And kept on scratching my face, with one hand. And screaming . . .*')

Scarfe fed coins into the slot, then talked to his daughter.

'That you, honey? . . . This is your father. Is Ralph around? . . . Good. I thought he'd be on duty. That's why I rang. Look, I want you to do me a favour. . . . Yes. Y'see, I don't want him to know I called. It's a bit delicate. Me being an alderman, y'see . . . But I've overheard something. Here, at the match. I'm calling from just outside the ground. Ralph should know. Tell him, when he comes home, this evening . . . It's about these break-ins he's working on. The stolen property. Some of it's going to be handed over to the receiver, this evening. . . . Yes, I know. But all sorts of people watch cricket matches, honey. Anyway, listen carefully. Ten o'clock, this evening. On the canal bank . . . Yes, there at Bordfield. On the canal bank about a quarter of a mile south of Brent Bridge . . . Brent Bridge, honey. There's some allotments there. That's where. . . . Oh, and tell him not to take anybody with him. They're very careful. Suspicious. Not to flood the place with policemen. I'd like to see him pull this off. It'll do him good in the force. If he's alone—I'd suggest alone—nobody can take the glory away from him, can they . . . That's right, honey . . . But don't tell him the information came from me . . . No, I'd say a woman. A woman's voice. Somebody with a grudge. Say that. Then he won't even guess . . . It'll do his career good. Bound to . . . Yes, I'll do that. Now, have you got all that clear? Ten o'clock, on the canal bank. Near the allotments, south of Brent Bridge . . . There's a good girl. See you tomorrow, when you come to pick up the kids . . . Look after yourself, honey.'

The man weighed the knife in the palm of his hand.

'A fine knife,' enthused the assistant. 'Just about the best of its kind on the market. We don't sell rubbish.'

It was, indeed, a fine knife and (for a split second) the thought flicked through the man's mind; what the hell legitimate purpose demanded such a cutting tool. It was almost twelve inches long, and eight of those inches were finest Sheffield steel. It had a flat, elongated triangular blade, the last two inches of which were shaped into a double-edged curve. The point was like a needle, and the cutting edge had been honed to razor-sharp perfection.

'About the finest hunting-knife on the market,' said the

assistant. 'It'll skin a deer—and, of course, lesser game—with no trouble at all.'

The hilt was of carved bone. Craftsman-carved, to fit snugly into the palm of a closed hand.

'Ten pounds, fifty,' murmured the assistant. 'As always, of course, if you're seeking the best you have to pay for the best.'

The man nodded, and passed the knife back to the assistant.

As the assistant re-sheathed the knife, the man peeled three five-pound notes from a bundle and passed them over the counter of the sports shop.

The assistant wrapped the knife carefully in brown paper, put the bank-notes into the drawer of the till, then handed the change back to the man.

He said, 'Thank you, sir. I'm sure you'll have nothing but satisfaction from that knife, sir.'

The man slipped the bundled knife into the inside pocket of his jacket. It was a little bulky—a little awkward—but, when he fastened the jacket, the package was completely hidden.

The woman relaxed in the comfort of one of the swivel wing rockers. She moved the chair gently, left and right. She rested her head against the back of the chair and gazed, unhappily, into the past. The immediate past. The immediate past . . . and the long-ago past.

The woman thought . . .
He isn't here. Tim isn't here. Nobody's here . . . just me. No fancy meal. No Sinatra making out-of-this-world music. Just me . . . and a decision.

Your decision, girl. The biggest decision you've made in your life. You can't have both. You can have either the toffee or the apple . . . but you can't have both.

Or neither!

Let's approach it. Let's pretend this is a story. Not life. Let's assume it's just one more manuscript. Let's pretend a little. Let's treat it as fiction; see what sort of an ending it needs. Happy ending? Unhappy ending? Open ending?

Open ending. They aren't too popular, these days. They so rarely come off. People are getting wise. Life isn't open-ended. Life has a beginning, a middle and . . . and this isn't a damn book, girl. This is life. So forget the thin ice and start asking yourself a few very pointed questions.

Question Number One. Can a woman love two men, at the same time? Forget the conventions, girl. Get back to nature. Get back to truth. Can she?

A husband and a son. A husband and a father. Uncles. Nephews. But, dammit, that's not the same thing. Two men. A man the law names as her husband and a man she names as her lover. Can she love them both simultaneously?

And, if not, why not? She can love two parents. She can love two children. She can love a father and a father-in-law. Why not the other thing? Why not the other kind of love?

Why not? . . . but that doesn't answer the question, that only asks it.

And, twelve years ago? Did you love him then? After what he'd done? Did you love him then?

No-o . . . you hated him then. At that moment, you hated him.

Or did you?

You're on your own, here, girl. You're digging deep for some sort of purity. Some sort of truth. Go to it. Dig really deep!

A rapist. What does a woman feel, when her husband's exposed as a rapist? Shame? . . . shame that her own body isn't enough, or isn't good enough? Shame at the realisation that she can't completely satisfy one man? And shame that her inadequacy is made public? Self-shame?

*Dig deeply enough, girl. You'll touch that vein of shame . . .
and that's the thing that triggers off the hatred. Wrap it
around with conventional disgust, and with expected horror.
That's expected. That's what 'civilisation' demands. But, what
about nature? What's the animal reaction?*

Shame. Self-reproach. Self-abasement.

*That's the sore spot, girl. That's what makes you cringe
away, when it's touched. But that's the truth . . . the first, tiny
truth you've ever handled in your whole life. So-o, get down.
Get onto your knees, and seek further. Shove your hand right
into the slime of subconsciousness. Go to it, girl—even if it
makes you puke—and answer the question.*

*Can a wife love a husband who's just been convicted of
rape?*

Scarfe was running low on coins. He left the kiosk, bought
cigarettes from a nearby tobacconist's, then returned to the
kiosk. He riffled through the yellow pages at the rear of the
directory, then dialled a number.

'Mrs. Lennox?'

'Speaking.'

'This is Alderman Scarfe here, Mrs. Lennox. I understand
you breed cats.'

'Russian Blues. Only Russian Blues.'

'Pedigree animals, of course.'

'Naturally.'

'I'm interested, Mrs. Lennox. For some time now, my wife
and I have contemplated introducing a cat into the household.'

'I see.'

'Various breeds. We've been advised on various breeds, my
wife seems taken with the idea of a Russian Blue.'

'I say nothing against the other breeds . . .'

'Quite.'

105

'. . . All cats are beautiful animals. But, in my opinion, the Russian Blue is, marginally, the best breed available.'

'Quite.'

'I have some kittens, if you're interested. You might like to call and look at them.'

'That's very handsome of you, Mrs. Lennox, and that's what I had in mind. Unfortunately, my work load limits the times when it would be possible.'

'Any time. At your own convenience, Mr—er . . .'

'Scarfe.'

'Mr. Scarfe.'

'I was thinking about this evening. Late evening . . . if that's possible.'

'Certainly. About what time?'

'Nine-thirty. Possibly a little after . . . but before ten. I know it's rather late, but . . .'

'Not at all. My husband's a policeman. He works all hours, and we rarely go out at night.'

'A policeman?'

'Yes. He comes in at . . .'

'Not Detective Chief Superintendent Lennox?'

'Yes. That's my husband.'

'Isn't that a coincidence. I know him. Not well . . . but, as a nodding acquaintance. I—er—I didn't know he bred cats as a hobby.'

'He doesn't. *I* breed them. And it's rather more than a hobby, Mr. Scarfe.'

'I beg your pardon, Mrs. Lennox. I didn't mean . . .'

'That's quite all right, Mr. Scarfe. I'll expect you this evening, then? At about half past nine.'

'If that's convenient.'

'Oh, yes. Quite convenient. I'll be expecting you.'

'Thank you, Mrs. Lennox.'

'Not at all, Mr. Scarfe. I'll see you then.'

Scarfe replaced the receiver.

As he stepped from the kiosk, the first spots of rain hit the pavement.

Tim Chambers stared from the window of his office, and watched the rain start. There was (he contemplated) something strangely *mechanical* about the start of a shower . . . as if it was the slipping into gear of a celestial engine. Slowly, at first. Then, gradually, gathering speed as the engine warmed up. Then a period of 'high speed cruising' . . . the period when the roofs ran water into the gutters; when the rain came down 'stair-rod' hard and soaked everything and everybody. Then the slowing; the gradual easing off of the accelerator—or, possibly, the screwing down of a valve—and, as smoothly as it had started, the engine came to rest, and the rain stopped.

Simple.

He sucked at his upper lip, and wished to hell *everything* was as simple.

He wished he could meet the man; this man who'd come from behind a prison wall and screwed up everybody's life. Not to hate him . . . who could hate a person who was only an occasionally-mentioned name? Not to fight him . . . good God Almighty (and even if he was an ex-con) the man must have some semblance of 'civilisation' left, and civilised men don't do battle for a woman. Just to meet him. To talk to him. To get to *know* him . . . if only a little.

It could be a cards-on-the-table meeting. Indeed, it would *have* to be a cards-on-the-table meeting; to be in love with another man's wife precluded any all-pals-together booze-up with the party concerned. Some straight talk, and some direct questions. Did he still love his wife? *Love* her? Not merely look upon her as a decorative bed-companion; as a soft touch, pending the arrival of better-times-around-the-corner.

Come to that, had he *ever* loved her?

To pick up a schoolkid, on his way home. To pull in at a lay-by and rape that schoolkid . . . and (presumably) hope to get away with it.

That pre-supposed a damn peculiar sort of 'love'.

Come to that, it pre-supposed a damn peculiar sort of *man.*

Oh, it happened. It was reported in the scandal rags every week. It happened all the time . . . but normal folk could never understand the 'why' of it all. Kinky types. Perverts. So, this man was (almost by definition) a pervert; he'd had money enough—a successful accountant, he'd not been without cash —and he could have paid for the services of a woman, had the need arose. But, he hadn't. Instead, he'd conned a school-kid into his car, then attacked her like an animal. Without doubt a pervert.

Which, in turn, meant . . .

Hell, turn it which way you liked, that made *her* the wife of a pervert. And, although her husband was a pervert, she couldn't make up her mind. Part of her wanted to go back to him. Part of her yearned to pick up, where they'd left off twelve years back.

To pick up *what?*

As he turned from the window he muttered, 'Oh God, *why?* Why can't you get inside another person's mind—really *inside*—and know what they *really* want?'

2.30 p.m. . . .

The woman still sat in the swivel wing rocker. Her efforts at self-examination had grown to be a near-physical fight with her inner self; it showed in her harsh, uncompromising expression and in the sheen of perspiration which had, already, broken through the thin mask of her make-up. She would never be the same person again . . . she knew that. She was, by any yardstick, an ordinary, efficient, moderately good-looking woman; she knew that . . . but she also knew that she (like every other ordinary, efficient, moderately good-looking woman—indeed, like *every* woman) carried a secret, and terrifying, 'other self' deep inside. This 'other self'. She'd clawed her way down, and reached it. She'd accepted it. Acknowledged it as a hidden part of herself; as a hidden part of every woman on earth.

The animal. The she-devil. The counterpart of brute-man.

The woman thought . . .
Original sin, girl. The ancients knew far more than they're ever credited with knowing. They wrapped it up in fancy language—allegorical language—and what they taught has been distorted beyond recognition . . . but they knew. They knew things the nut-doctors of today are still a hundred miles from knowing. A million miles from understanding.

Can a wife love a husband who's just been convicted of rape?

She can, girl. She can . . . and you know why she can. You know the basic savage reason. The reason that's always there, but never admitted, because to admit it would be a rejection of a few hundred years of imposed 'civilised' pressure. The reason which, if admitted, would brand you as a savage.

Take love—take hatred—accept them, as the mix that they are. And the hatred you had for him, twelve years ago, wasn't a hatred for him. It was directed at him, because convention insisted that it be directed at him. Oh, the hatred was there, all right. It was a hatred born of its first cousin, jealousy . . . or, perhaps, envy. But it was a hatred of her!

No . . . not because she was a hot-arsed little cow. Not because she'd opened her legs and offered him something he couldn't resist. Not (if he's to be believed) because she was too sexy to resist.

109

Steady, girl. Steady—but admit it . . . because she'd been raped.

The animal . . . right? The basic urge . . . right? The deep-down yearning of every woman, to be 'taken', by force . . . right?

A husband, who's a rapist. The imagination . . . yours had run riot, girl. Admit it. Admit it, if only to yourself. And, you were angry. But—although the anger was directed towards him—it was an anger based upon something far more fundamental than disgust.

It was an anger built on jealousy. On envy. On the secret desire to have been that young tart . . . to have been raped, by your own husband.

Don't puke at the thought, girl.

It's true . . . and you know it.

You were angry at him. You were blazing mad at him. But for that reason. And, because of that, it was an anger incapable of destroying love. God help us, it was an anger that increased the love for him you already had.

So-o, can a wife love a husband who's just been convicted of rape?

You bet your sweet life she can! It's a secret love—it's a love with a spice of envy, a hint of anger, and a whole taste of promise . . . but, it's a bigger love than ever.

Get with it, girl. We're animals . . . that's your answer.

The woman lowered her head, cupped her face in her hands and indulged in the luxury of a long, shuddering sigh. She stood up from the swing wing rocker and walked, a little unsteadily, across the room to where the boxed cigarettes and the lighter stood on the side-table.

She felt drained. Drained of all emotion, drained of all energy, drained of all desire.

It had been one hell of a session, and the truth sat, like a huge black boulder, squarely across her shoulders.

As she lighted the trembling cigarette, she wondered how she was going to break the news to Tim.

As Scarfe strolled into his shop the man, Charterouse, looked up with surprise, and said, 'Oh, hello Mr. Scarfe. I thought you were . . .'

'A poor match,' grunted Scarfe. 'It wasn't worth watching.' He waved his hand, and continued, 'I'm not stopping. I just thought I'd call in, on the way home. Check things were running smoothly.'

'Oh, yes . . . the police,' murmured Charterhouse. 'Your son-in-law, Chief Inspector Finney, called.'

'Really?'

'Something about a tip-off. That they've heard a rumour that the shop might be burgled.'

'Is that a fact?' Scarfe raised inquisitive eyebrows.

'Nothing definite, Mr. Scarfe. He just wanted to check the stock, and the alarm systems.'

'And?'

'He seemed quite satisfied. He inspected the strong-room. He said he'll contact you, about the safe.'

'Ah!'

'I told him . . . you're the only key-holder, sir. He understood.'

'Ye-es, of course. I'll ring him when I get home.'
Charterhouse nodded.

'That's it, then.' Scarfe glanced around the shop. 'No problems? . . . other than that?'

'No, sir.' Charterhouse smiled. 'Everything under control.'

Scarfe returned the smile, and said, 'Fine. I'll see you Monday.'

'Yes, sir.'

Scarfe walked out of the shop and closed the door.

('. . . I didn't tear the shirt, or the shorts. That's what I'm getting at. They weren't torn. Neither of them. Not when the officer arrived at the car. The Scarfe girl was still screaming. Still scratching. She was still screaming that she was being raped. But, she wasn't. I swear, she wasn't.

'Then the officer arrived, and opened the car door. And, before I had time to say anything, he leaned inside. Leaned across me, and ripped her shirt. Ripped it badly . . . that was what was shown at court. He ripped her shorts . . . they were shown at court. Then—after that—he asked what was going on.'

'A set-up,' rumbled Lennox. 'That's what you're saying, is it? A deliberate set-up.'

'I didn't rape her. Keep morals out of it, and I didn't do anything she didn't want me to do.'

'It's your story, son. Tell it in your own way.'

'I think he knew her. The constable from the police car. I think he knew who she was . . . and that maybe she knew him. That's the impression I had. They didn't say anything. Either of them. They denied it, in court, but I think they were lying.'

'Just the one copper?' grunted Lennox.

'That's—that's what I thought. There should have been two, shouldn't there? A squad car. There's always . . .'

'Not always. Usually. Sometimes one of 'em isn't around. Off sick. On holiday. Usually two . . . but not always.'

'Oh! Well, there was only one, this time. And he fixed it. He tore the clothes . . . not me. Then, he wouldn't let me talk, while she told a pack of lies. Then . . .'

The tape-recorder spool revolved, and Lennox resumed his attitude of a bored and half-sleep Buddah.)

The man stood up from his seat. He made his way down the centre aisle of the swaying carriage; 'walking' his hands from seat-back to seat-back to keep his balance. At the toilet, between the two carriages, he entered and shot the bolt of the door.

Bracing himself against the lip of the washbasin, he removed his jacket and hung it on the hook provided by British Rail for such purposes. Then he unbuttoned his shirt, and hung that on top of his jacket.

From the side pocket of his jacket he took out the leather belt he'd bought, at the shop within a stone's throw of the station. From the inside pocket of his jacket he took out the knife.

He removed the wrappings, then threaded the belt through the thong of the knife's sheath. Then, he positioned the belt across his right shoulder, diagonally across his chest, and fixed the buckle to allow the knife's hilt to end about nine inches below his left armpit. The tip of the sheath hung a good inch lower than his waistband.

He took his shirt from the hook, threaded his arms through the sleeves and buttoned it up the front, without tucking it into the top of his trousers.

He turned, to check things in the mirror above the washbasin.

He settled the knife into a comfortable position, under the shirt, then pinched the cloth of the shirt at the point where the hilt of the knife ended and the sheath began. Using first one hand, then the other, he kept the cloth pinched, unbuttoned the shirt and slipped it clear of his arms.

Then, one-handed, he removed the blade from its housing, he slit the cloth, carefully, where it was pinched.

He placed the knife on the floor of the toilet before fixing his shirt into position once more and, this time, unhooking the waistband of his trousers and tucking shirt, and the last inch or so of the sheath, into position. He fastened the waistband, stooped, picked up the knife and, threading the blade through the slit in the cloth, housed it in the sheath. He settled the arrangement into a comfortable position.

He put on his jacket and examined the result in the mirror.

The sheath of the knife was completely hidden. There wasn't even a bulge. With the jacket fastened, nobody could see a thing. Even with the jacket open, unless the front flew wide, nobody could see the hilt of the knife.

But it was there. Ready to hand . . . like a short sword, handy for any trouble which might arise.

He fastened his jacket, washed his hands, screwed up the wrappings and dropped them into the used-towel bin, unlocked the door and made his way back to his seat.

'Call that it,' grunted Finney. 'It's Saturday . . . what's left can wait for Monday.'

Holmes said, 'They're still on house-to-house.'

Finney moved his shoulders.

'Call *them* off too?'

'To do what?'

'Some have had a long spell.'

'They're *here* to do long spells.'

'There's some paper-work to catch up with.'

'Leave 'em, sergeant,' said Finney. 'They're keeping the customers happy.'

'Still,' insisted Holmes, 'if you think it's Scarfe.'

'It's Scarfe.'

'In that case . . .'

'The fence. I want the lifter, too. I want the whole bloody bun, Holmes . . . not just the cherry from the top. Maybe Scarfe'll cough. I doubt it . . . he'll have some crappy solicitor at his elbow, before we even touch his collar. You never know . . . the house-to-house rigmarole might turn some stone and send some little bug scurrying into the open.'

'The thief?'

'The bun, *and* the cherry,' repeated Finney.

Holmes smiled, ruefully.

'It'll come,' said Finney, confidently. 'Spread the manure thick enough, and something always grows. Meanwhile, take time off. Let the donkeys do the donkey-work. Come Monday, *we* start being nasty.'

3 p.m. . . .

Scarfe asked, 'Where's the kids?'

'Out in the garden.' His wife looked up, flush-faced from where she was positioning dishes and plates in the oven. She closed the door, straightened and held a hand to the small of her back, as the twinge of oncoming age touched her.

'It's raining. They'll catch cold,' complained Scarfe.

'In the shed. Cowboys and Indians . . . by the sound of things.'

'Good.' Scarfe chuckled. 'I'll join 'em.'

His wife brushed a stray lock of greying hair from the front of her eye, and warned, 'Don't get too rough. They get excited, then they can't get off to sleep, at bedtime.'

'Bedtime? It's hours before . . .'

'Just don't get them too excited. That's all.'

Scarfe hurried from the kitchen and into the rear garden. He ran down the concrete path, to clear the rain before it soaked him.

His grandchildren greeted him with squeals of high delight.

The truth was, he loved these kids. Their innocence fascinated him the more, each time he encountered it; their blind acceptance that the world was a nice place, inhabited by nice people; that bogey-men were only an offshoot of fairies and Father Christmas, there to send delicious shivers down the spine, but never to be taken too seriously.

Alderman Frank Scarfe romped and played with his grandchildren. He made them laugh and gave them joy; they loved this great, jovial grandfather of theirs.

And, contradictory though it may seem, the truth was that he returned their love in full . . . despite the fact that he'd arranged for the slaughter of their father.

3.10 p.m. . . .

The man shrugged the plastic mac onto his shoulders and hurried from the graffiti-scrawled hall of Leeds City Station.

Leeds. 'The Motorway City'. A very wet and miserable-looking 'motorway city' at the moment. The Black Prince, arm extended and finger pointing accusingly, sat astride his horse and dripped rain and pigeon droppings; a landmark and the centre-piece of City Square . . . a city mascot, and no more than that, because what the hell the Prince of Aquitaine and Gascony had in common with a dump which was little more than a cluster of mud huts, at the time, has long slipped the memory of history.

But, The Black Prince and City Square and, dodging the traffic, the man hurried along, past the statue and towards the Town Hall; towards the ring of 'city boozers' which encircled the shops and offices; hopefully, towards some stranger who might point him in the direction of a villain called Conboy . . . and a gun.

3.30 p.m. . . .

Finney said, 'I'm hungry. What is there?'

'It's a funny time,' complained Myra Finney, sulkily.

'I'm a funny man.'

'Half-way between lunch and dinner.'

'Lunch? Dinner?' sneered Finney.

'What's that supposed to mean?'

'All that fancy food-talk.'

'So?'

'You couldn't put a decent meal on, if your life hung on it.' She turned, blazed her eyes at him, and snapped, 'All right ... try somebody else.'

'What the hell?' Finney stared, slack-mouthed, at his angry wife.

'Your spare piece,' she rasped.

'*What* spare piece?'

'Let that little cow feed you.'

'*WHAT SPARE PIECE?*' bawled Finney.

'Think I don't know?'

'I don't even know what the bloody hell you're *talking* about.'

'Think I can't *tell*?'

'Look—all I said was that I'm ...'

'Think a wife doesn't *know* these things?'

'*What* bloody things?'

'You're useless. That's how I know ... 'cos you're *useless*.'

'Hold it, right there,' warned Finney, harshly.

'In bed. You're bloody useless.'

'Of all the damn ...'

'You never were *much* good. But, these days ...'

Myra Finney ended whatever insult she was about to hurl with a yelp of pain. Finney's open palm smacked across her cheek, full-muscled, turned her on her heels and sent her sprawling into one of the armchairs. Finney stood over her. His eyes blazed near-uncontrollable fury and his voice matched the upsurge of rage.

'Right,' he snarled. 'We'll have it, shall we? Act and bloody section. Four letter words, we can both understand.'

'You've got another woman,' she panted.

'Who says so?' The question was accompanied by a second hard slap across the face.

'You think I don't know? You think a wife doesn't *know*?

When you can't even get a hard on, because some other bitch
has...'

The slaps came fast and furious. Non-stop. Full-blooded
swings which rocked her head from left to right. She tried to
turn in the chair; tried to scramble free of the punishment by
kneeling with her back to him on the seat of the chair. He
grabbed the top of her skirt, to yank her back, and the cloth
tore and the skirt came away in his hands. He flung the ruined
skirt aside and fastened his grip on her shoulder, spun her
round and continued the beating.

The chair almost toppled backwards, righted itself ... and
still he slapped. She held her hands up her face, to ward off
the blows, and he closed his fist around the material of her
blouse and tore it free, like so much gossamer.

She wasn't yelping any more.

He stood back, panting and, slowly, she lowered her hands.
Huddled in the chair, as she was, wearing only a strip of a
brassière and pink mini-panties trimmed with black lace.

A tiny trickle of blood seeped from one corner of her mouth
and crept towards her chin, but her eyes gradually lost their
fear. Instead, they took on a faraway, dazed look; a dreamy
look, with wildness in their depths.

'You bitch,' he breathed. 'You bloody *slut*!'

'Strip me,' she whispered, and her voice was a hoarse echo
of past memories.

'You cow.'

'Strip me ... *please*!'

He was trembling slightly as he muttered, 'I'll bloody *kill*
you.'

He reached forward, closed his fingers around the slip of
cloth which linked the cups of the brassière and jerked her
forward. He met her chin with the heel of the other hand and,
although the straps bit deep into her skin, before they snapped,
her bloodied mouth curved into a slow smile of triumph.

She fell back into the chair and arched her middle, as if offering the last garment for vandalisation.

He panted, 'You bloody cow,' as he gripped the top of her panties, dragged her from the armchair and spun her, face downwards, sprawling on the hearth-rug. The breath was knocked from her body, but she twisted to stare up at him. Naked. Fighting for breath. Then writhing as the first orgasm hit her, and as he tore himself free from his own clothes.

'Anything,' she gasped. 'Anything. The kids aren't here . . . *anything!*'

('. . . And, at the trial, it was a foregone conclusion. They dressed her up. They made her look so young. So innocent. She sounded so convincing. I hadn't a hope. They both lied. She and the policeman. They took the oath, and they both committed perjury. They killed any possible plea of mitigation.'

There was a silence, then Lennox raised his head, and said, 'Eighteen years, wasn't it?'

'A vicious sentence.'

'I ain't allowed to make comment, sonny.'

'A third off, for good conduct.' There was contempt in the words.

'Twelve years is a long time,' grunted the fat detective.

'You don't know how long. Nobody knows how long . . . until they end the sentence. Then, there's a re-birth.'

Lennox took a pouch from his pocket and began to stuff shredded tobacco into the bull's-head bowl of his pipe. He concentrated all his attention upon what appeared, to him, to be a complicated operation.

'A re-birth.' The repetition of the two words sounded like an attempt at self-conviction.

'The penologists reckon four years,' observed Lennox.

'Four years?'

'After that, what goes in don't come out.'

'Prison is a lunatic answer. It's an admission of failure.'

'I've heard the argument, son.' Lennox blew into the pipe, to test for draught. *'There might be summat in it . . . I wouldn't know.'*

'To cage a man up, because he's made a mistake?'

'Sonny,' said Lennox, grimly, *'I wouldn't call what some of 'em do "mistakes".'*

'Many! Many!' The low-spoken words were like a savage litany; learned, repeated and carrying absolute faith. *'So many men who have weakened. Weak men, who only need the strength of understanding. Men who are ill. Sick men, who need expert treatment. Not bad men. Not evil men. But they're all lumped together under the single heading "criminal". They're all locked away, together. The weak, the sick and the evil. They all come out tainted. Not cured—none of them are cured . . . they're merely tainted.'*

Lennox wheezed a little as he hauled himself to his feet. He glanced at the tape-recorder, pressed the 'stop' button and said, 'We need a new reel. Settle back, son. Have a fag, while I go fetch one.')

4.15 p.m. . . .

The rain wove da Vinci patterns as it ran in the gutters, and gurgled as it cascaded into the drains; it was silver, against the gunmetal of the July sky and, as it veneered the tarmac of the roads, it mirrored the colours of the city. At Harrogate, play had long been abandoned; the players haring for the shelter of the pavilion as the first drizzle had wound itself up into a steady downpour. In a garden shed, a man and his three grandchildren watched the slanting streaks, felt warm and safe in their secret shelter and wagered sweets with each other upon the speed of droplets sliding down the outer surface of the window. In Leeds a man felt the dampness soak through the material of his trouser legs, as the rain dripped from the edge of a plastic mac. And, on the outskirts of Bordfield—in a house called 'White Gates', in a half-circle of houses called Raymon Crescent—a naked man, and a naked woman, sprawled, exhausted, in twin armchairs and were quite oblivious to the weather.

Tim Chambers opened the door of his bachelor apartment, in answer to the ring, stared, then gasped, 'Good God, you're soaked. Come inside.'

'It wasn't raining when I set out.' The woman's hair was in sodden rat-tails; the jacket of her two-piece was dark-stained and saturated; her shoes squelched water as she passed him and walked into the hall. She said, 'I'm—I'm sorry if I'm making a mess.'

As he closed the door, he said, 'You've *walked*?'

'Yes.'

'In this lot?'

'It wasn't . . .'

'For heaven's sake, get those things off.' He cupped her elbow in his hand and guided her into the apartment. 'You know where the bathroom is. Have a good soak. I'll leave pyjamas and dressing-gown on the bed.'

'Tim, I have to . . .'

'Later! You're *begging* for pneumonia. Now—don't argue . . . I'll be waiting in the lounge.'

'Please, Tim . . .'

'No arguments. Do as I say.'

She felt like weeping. She felt like a child, again; not being scolded for misbehaviour, but being pampered by an anxious and loving parent. He was like that. That was the depth of his affection—that was the manner of his affection—that was the great strength of his affection but, at the same time, its weakness . . . and the realisation almost broke her heart.

*

Myra Finney muttered, 'A woman phoned.'

Finney scowled, and grunted, 'Don't start *that* again.'

'No. Some sorta message.'

'What message?'

'A case. Are you on a case?'

'I'm *always* on a case, for Christ's sake.'

'She—er—she didn't give her name. Just a tip-off.'

'Go on.' Finney roused himself enough to show some slight interest.

'About some break-ins.'

'Aye?'

'Are you having some break-ins, then?'

'Aye. What about 'em?' Finney hoisted himself from the armchair, rescued his underpants from behind the chair and hauled them up his tree-trunk thick legs. As he flopped back into the chair, he growled, 'All right. What was the tip?'

'That the—er—thief is going to hand the property over to the receiver, tonight.'

'I've heard 'em,' sneered Finney.

'What?'

'Those sorta tip-offs. Scores of times.'

'Well, that's what . . .'

'Anonymous . . . right?'

'Er—yes. She—er—she didn't give her name.'

'It's all ballocks,' pronounced Finney, flatly.

'I—I don't think so.'

'What the hell do you know about these things?'

'The—the voice. It sounded . . .'

'They all do.'

'What?'

Finney said, 'The crawlers. The snouts who haven't the guts to come into the open. Oh, they sound convincing . . . *bloody* convincing. Over a telephone. But, face-to-face. They get a kick outa sending tired coppers on wild-goose chases. That's about what it boils down to.'

'This one sounded very . . .'

'Why here?' demanded Finney. 'Why not phone the nick? Why not get me at the office? Forget it . . . it stinks.'

Myra Finney hesitated, then said, 'Look . . . it wasn't a woman.'

'Eh?'

'He said I had to *say* it was a woman.'

'*That's* a new gag.'

'It was . . .' She moistened her lips, then said, 'It was father.'

'*Your* father?' Finney widened his eyes.

She nodded.

'Then, why the hell . . .'

'He said he didn't want dragging into it.'

'Oh, aye?'

'Him being an alderman . . . y'see.'

'Oh, aye. Him being an *alderman*.'

'That's why he told me to say it was a woman.'

Finney scratched the top of his leg, then reached under his backside, pulled free the string vest he was sitting on and threaded his arms through the sleeves.

He growled, 'Well . . . go on. What else?'

'Tonight, at about ten o'clock.'

'What?'

'The thief's going to hand the stuff over to the receiver.'

'As definite as that . . . eh?' He leaned forward, picked his socks from the hearthrug and yanked them onto his feet. 'Owt else?'

'On the towpath. Up by the canal.'

'That's where, is it?'

'Yes.'

'Nice to know.'

'About a quarter of a mile from Brent Bridge. There's some allotments.'

'I know 'em.'

'There. That's where it's gonna happen.'

'At ten o'clock?'

'That's what father said.'

His shirt had been thrown onto the sofa. Finney reached for it, straightened it and pulled the sleeves over his arms.

As he fastened the buttons, he said, 'All this info. Where did *he* get it? Did he say?'

'At the match. He phoned from a booth, outside the ground.'

'Oh, aye?'

'He'd heard somebody talking. Thought you should know.'

'At the match?'

'That's where he heard it.'

'You hear some bloody funny remarks at a cricket match,' observed Finney, drily.

'Meaning you're gonna ignore it.'

'Oh, no.' Finney reached for his trousers and pulled them up to his waist. He said, 'From an *alderman*. I mean . . . you can't ignore a tip-off from an *alderman*. Don't worry. I'll be there. With knobs on.'

4.30 p.m. . . .

The man said, 'I want a w-word with Conboy.'

'Yeah?' The bruiser, despite the waiter's uniform, still looked a bruiser; only plastic surgery would alter the slightly flattened nose, or take the scar-tissue from above the left eye. This boy had slugged bloody battles with fellow-cruiserweights, and had marks to prove it. He was a few years too old for the game, these days—a few years too old, and just a mite punchy —but the strain on the uniform's seams was proof that the

124

basic machinery of the fight racket was still all there, and in working order. He said, 'Who's callin', anyway?'

The man took a deep breath, then said, 'Tell him "the k-kid-screwer" . . . he'll know.'

'It don't make sense.' The bruiser picked his battered nose, reflectively. 'He don't like strangers interruptin'. And that name don't make sense.'

'It will to him.'

'And, if it don't?'

The ghost smile touched the man's mouth, as he said, 'Th-then you'll bounce me.'

'Yeah.' The bruiser nodded solemn agreement. 'Then, I'll bounce you, buster.'

The bruiser turned and ambled his way across the thick pile of the empty restaurant.

It was a top-class eating-house; deserted in the dead period between lunch and dinner, but with polished-top tables, orange coloured place-mats, good cutlery and folded, foolscap-size menues. A hors-d'oeuvre trolley stood in one corner, alongside a giant-sized side-board-cum-hot-plate. From beyond the swingdoors, leading to the kitchens, somebody was whistling a slightly out-of-tune version of *Sleepy-Time Gal*, to the accompaniment of rattling pans and running water.

The man unbuttoned the plastic mac, and waited.

Tim Chambers thought she looked like a frightened child and, indeed, she *did*. The sweet little orphan of the storm, with her damp hair wrapped in a towel turban; wearing pyjamas a few sizes too large beneath a terry-cloth dressing-gown. Minus makeup, minus every last vestige of 'sophistication' and curled, like a timid animal, in the comfort of the leather wing-chair. Staring at the glow from the triple-bar electric fire, with eyes deadened by an almost forgotten past, a miserable present and an unknown future.

'It's over,' she said, sadly, and her voice was as faraway as her eyes.

Chambers flipped a cigarette case open, chose two cigarettes, placed them both between his lips, lighted them, then handed one across to her.

She took it, quietly, and with a slow, somnambulistic movement, drew on it, then said, 'He's my husband. I can't divorce him. I can't two-time him. It's over, Tim . . . I had to let you know.'

'Uhu.' He nodded, as if comforting a worried child.

'You don't believe it?'

'No.' He smiled. 'I don't believe it.'

'It's true.' She turned her head, slowly, and looked at him. 'It's true, Tim. It *has* to be.'

'He's always been your husband. Ever since we met . . . all that time, he's been your husband, darling. And, all that time, you've been "two-timing" him. You can't suddenly have an attack of conscience . . . just like that.'

She drew on the cigarette. Jerkily, and without inhaling.

She said, 'Until today, I hadn't a choice.'

'Not true,' he murmured.

'He wasn't around.'

'He was *there*. The marriage was still valid. He was going to *be* around . . . eventually. But, you didn't even visit him.'

'I was disgusted.'

'And now you're not?'

'When it happened, I was ashamed of him . . . *for* him.'

'And now, you're not ashamed?'

'You wouldn't understand,' she said, dully.

'Try me.'

'He's my husband.'

'No!' He spoke gently, but firmly. '*I'm* your husband. Never mind the piece of paper. Never mind the legal formalities. Today, *I'm* your husband . . . far more than he is.'

'I wish . . .' she began, sadly, then stopped.

'What? That I was?'

'That you *had* been. Twelve years ago.'

'I still can be. Believe me . . . it's possible. Even easy.'

'You—you haven't seen him.'

'I don't give a damn about him. I'm sorry . . . but he screwed himself into the dung-heap, twelve years ago. That's a fact. Face it. And, for God's sake, don't ask me to feel sorry for him now.'

'I'm not asking you to feel . . .'

'And don't hide behind all that "you-don't-understand" rubbish. I understand. I'm a grown man . . . I understand, perfectly.' Some of the gentleness in his tone was replaced by impatience. He leaned forward, slightly, in his chair, placed a hand on each knee, and said, 'The villains always get the best lines . . . remember. In every play, in every book, in every motion picture. The villain always gets the best lines. It happens in life, too. They always get the best women. Scoundrels fascinate good women. Don't ask me why . . . they just *do*.'

'That's a ridiculous thing to . . .'

'Ridiculous—yes . . . but *true*.' For the first time, she heard something akin to anger and disgust in his words. 'Show me an absolute louse, and I'll put a fiver on the table that somewhere there's a good woman who dotes on him. Who's forever excusing him. Forgiving him. Pretending he's something he isn't, and never will be. Look, my pet, the great writers all knew this. They traded on this illogical weakness of women. Take Dickens . . . most women like Dickens. And which characters do they like best? Which characters do they remember? Scrooge. Sikes. Fagin. The Artful Dodger. *Those* sort of characters. All right . . . they all either got their just deserts, or reformed, in the end, but that's not important. As *characters*, they were evil . . . and women love them.

Rochester, in *Jane Eyre*. Shakespeare's *Hamlet*. Even today—Fleming's James Bond . . . the last word in the love-'em-and-leave-'em brigade. Look at them. Inconsiderate. Selfish. Arrogant. Sometimes, downright rotten. Fictitious—okay, fictitious . . . but, dream creatures adored by thousands of simpering, illogical women. Women of all ages.'

She stared at the bars of the electric fire, and muttered, 'That's not fair. That's not . . .'

'Fair! Who's talking about being "fair"?'

'You've no right to . . .'

'Shut up!' The flash of anger died and, in a more reasonable voice he said, 'Shut up, darling. Listen. Listen, because I *have* the right. More right than he has. More right than he's ever had. To you, he may be your husband but, to me, he's just another man. A man who's trying to take you away from me. A man who's playing upon your weaknesses . . . not just *your* weaknesses, every woman's weaknesses. The weakness of imagining she can tame any, and every, brute she comes across.'

The woman thought . . .

Darling Tim, you're so right. You're so right, and you're so wise. The wisdom of a good man, who isn't blind to the rottenness of the world. The wisdom to understand women. I hadn't realised . . . it's so very rare.

You know so much that other men don't.

The pop groups. Use them as your argument, Tim darling. I'm no screaming teenager. I'm a woman—almost a middle-aged woman—but I know the feeling, because I've been to some of the concerts. I've seen the screaming, swooning hordes. I've known what they've felt. I've understood.

The groups, too. God, what psychology! So good—so complete—it's hypnotic.

The deliberate phallic symbolism of the guitars. The skin-tight trousers, cut and tailored to emphasise the mound made by the stinkhorn of procreation; moulded and glorified in expensive, gaudy colouring. The exaggerated writhing and jerking; the over-acted mockery of sexual contortions. And the words—the hidden meanings, and secret promises, of the words . . . and the blubber-lipped, sensuous manner of their delivery.

And, the make-up. My God, the make-up! The art of profanity, in colour and style. Youth, deliberately clothed and masked in sin itself.

They aren't bad kids . . . the majority. Nor are their howling followers bad kids . . . the majority. But, show-biz has learned what you already know, Tim, darling.

That the story of Eve and the apple is a great and ancient truth. That, of the two sexes, woman is by far the more sinful. Very few men are whores. Very few men tantalise, or tease, for the sheer thrill of power. Very few men strip their bodies naked in the craft of mass, pseudo-seduction.

The make-believe? The mockery? The lie?

That women are the 'pure ones'; that only men have exotic fantasies.

The lies are masked by centuries of practised hypocrisy . . . but, beneath the hypocrisy the truth bubbles and smoulders, like a volcano fighting to erupt.

Watch the teenagers, slack-mouthed and screaming, at a pop concert. Count the masturbators, eager-eyed and waiting at countless 'massage parlours'. Woman . . . she is carnality, personified, Tim, darling. She is forever Eve, the temptress. She represents excess and debauchery.

All women—every woman—and take no heed of her denial . . . the denial is the very keystone of her guile. Her denial is her shield; it protects her from man's disgust; it counters his accusation, before the accusation is even made, and makes him carry the guilt which, in reality, is hers.

All this, you suspect, Tim, darling. All this you half-know . . . which makes you a uniquely wise man. Go the whole hog,

*then. Take that last, logical step into the filth and mystery of
a woman's mind, and know that you can't win.*

To be possessed by a rapist!

*The thought—the mere thought—affects me. I don't love
him—not as I love you . . . but I need him. I yearn for him.
I want him . . . I want him so badly, it's almost driving me
out of my mind.*

To be possessed by a rapist!

*The secret dream of every woman in the world . . . and I
have the legal right to turn that dream into reality.*

Tim, darling . . . you haven't a cat in hell's chance.

4.45 p.m. . . .

'You are not the lovely boy you used to be, Joey,' grinned
Conboy.

The man hated him with his eyes. This Conboy; this one-
time block boss, with his fixed grin and everlasting perversions.

The grin stayed in position, as Conboy said, 'You're looking
older than last time, Joey. You've worn badly.'

'I don't like that name,' said the man, quietly.

'Joey?'

'It's not a nice name.'

'You're not a nice man, pal. Come to that, I wouldn't even
call you a *man* . . . Joey.'

The man nodded slow resignation, and unslipped the button
of his jacket from its button-hole.

He said, 'I was told you could help me, Conboy.'

'*Me*? Help *you*?' The grin expanded into a shoulder-
shaking chuckle.

'I was told.'

'You are way beyond help, pal. You're no mug. You know
these things. All the kids are safe from you now, Joey.'

The office was carpeted and furnished in immaculate taste.

It was dumb evidence of good living; positive proof that crime, if organised on a big enough scale, not only paid, but paid well. Block boss. That, by simple, criminal definition had meant 'big time'; a man with 'connections'; a man with power; a man with the façade of respectability, provided by a fine restaurant and a beautiful office. A man like Conboy.

'I need a gun, Conboy,' said the man, softly.

Conboy's grin expanded.

'A gun,' repeated the man, flat-toned and tired-voiced. 'A pistol. A revolver. I don't mind which. A gun and bullets.'

'I run an eating-house, pal. Not a gun-shop.'

'You run other things, too.'

'Let us not get personal, Joey.'

'You were a king rat inside, Conboy.'

'You *are* getting personal, pal.' The grin stayed, but the eyes glittered warnings.

The man ignored the warnings and continued, 'King rat, inside. King rat, outside. You can get me a gun, Conboy. I'll pay.'

Conboy eased his thick body back a little. He was sitting behind the massive, polished-topped desk, with its silver pen-stand, its mock-Victorian telephone, its tooled-leather blotter. He eased back in his chair and unobtrusively dropped a hand from the surface of the desk, to one of the drawer handles.

The man made-believe not to notice and hooked the thumb of his right hand into the waistband of his trousers.

'Name the price,' said the man, gently.

'On your way, Joey,' grinned Conboy. 'Walk, before terrible things happen to you.'

'More terrible things?' The wraith-smile touched sad lips, then disappeared.

'You've found guts from somewhere, pal.' The fingers slid open one of the drawers. 'Lose 'em, before they buy you a whole lot of misery.'

'I came here for a gun.'

'You've had a wasted journey, pal. This is . . .'

There was speed; eye-defeating speed. Conboy slipped the revolver from the desk drawer as the man closed his fist on the hilt of the hunting knife and drew the heavy blade from its sheath. It was like a short sword—like a cleaver biting, bone-deep into meat—and the hand holding the revolver spurted blood and was pinned to the desk top, before the finger could find the trigger.

The grin was no longer there. Eyes met eyes, and the eyes of Conboy showed the fear.

'You made me what I am, Conboy,' whispered the man. 'Don't complain. You did a fine job.'

He held the blade hard in the flesh and, with his free hand, eased the blood-stained revolver from the useless fingers.

'You're a dead man, pal,' breathed Conboy.

'Not before you.' The man glanced at the surface of the desk; at the growing, swimming blood which bubbled from the front of Conboy's wrist. He said, 'That's an artery, Conboy. Hope the ambulance service has some good drivers. And, if this gun's been used for killing, take advice . . . don't mention my name.'

The man slipped the revolver into the left-hand pocket of the plastic mac. In a single, hate-filled movement, he jerked the blade from Conboy's wrist and swung it in a left-to-right slash across the gangster's face; biting into flesh, bone and nose-cartilage and disfiguring for life.

Conboy's chair toppled and he sprawled on the carpet.

As he hurried from the office, the man re-sheathed the knife and buttoned-up the plastic mac.

(*The new spool rotated and, once more, the words were recorded.*

Lennox grunted, 'Okay, son. It's all yours.'

'I want to talk.'

'Go ahead.' Lennox flicked at a lighter, but the spark refused to make a flame.

'Not just a monologue.' There was quiet desperation somewhere deep inside the tone. 'I mean talk . . . with somebody.'

'A solicitor?' Lennox discarded the lighter and sought matches.

'I don't need a solicitor.'

'Anybody in particular?'

'You.'

'I'm a policeman, sonny.' Lennox scratched a match against the side of its box, then held the flame to the bull's-head bowl of his ridiculous pipe. He puffed clouds of evil smelling smoke, as he rumbled, 'That's a detail you have to remember. Me being a policeman. You being . . . just what would you say you are, son?'

'I'm an ex-con. You know that, already.'

As he waved out the match, Lennox remarked, 'You say it all wrong.'

'What's that?'

' "Ex-con". You don't sound convincing enough, old son.'

'It's what I am.'

'Like a new recruit saying he's a copper. He ain't . . . not yet.'

'All right. I'm a convicted rapist. Is that enough?'

'For me.' Lennox shrugged. 'You ain't likely to shock me, son, if that's what you're after.'

'Twelve years.' There was a dreamy, sing-song quality about the word.

'Aye.' The obese detective puffed at his pipe and nodded. 'There's a nice interesting subject for chit-chat. Those twelve years . . . what makes 'em so special?'

'Have you ever been to prison?'

Lennox chuckled and shook his head.

'It's a hell of a sentence.'

'Men have served longer . . . without talking about it as much.'

'What the hell do you know . . .'

'Hold it, old son.' Lennox waved the stem of his pipe, reprovingly. 'Decide which horse you're going to ride. Ex-con, ex-rapist . . . or the indignant bloke who was framed by the naughty coppers.'

'Sorry.' The whisper of an embarrassed smile accompanied the apology. 'Can I smoke again?'

'I'm smoking. Why not you?'

Cigarette smoke joined the tobacco smoke, and a fug began to build up in Number Three Interview Room.)

5 p.m. . . .

Tim Chambers carried her into the bedroom, lowered her onto the bed and worked the terry-cloth dressing-gown from her limp body. He eased her legs clear, then turned down the nylon sheet and eiderdown. He positioned her comfortably before covering her with the bedclothes.

Chloral hydrate—trade name 'Noctec'—okay, it was something the man-in-the-street couldn't even buy with a doctor's prescription . . . but modern electronics needed the scientific know-how of a lot of people, and some of those people included scientists with an expertise in chemistry. And, for 'knock-out drops'—for something that *really* dumped you in Dreamland, irregardless of all and every worry of the day— chloral hydrate was in a class apart. 'Noctec' . . . these boys could, if the request came from a high enough level, reach under the counter and procure a little for directors, and such.

Tim Chambers was no great advocate of drugs. Any sort of drugs. But, some six months previously, he'd needed rest, and rest had refused to come. The answer had been chloral hydrate. 'Noctec'. With *very* careful instructions from the friend who'd provided the stuff.

The truth was, it had scared the hell out of him; it had been like being smacked across the back of the neck with a trip-hammer . . . the action had been *that* fast!

Tim Chambers didn't regret what he'd done.

She was the woman in his life (*the* woman in his life) and, if ever a person had needed the balm of quick, recuperative sleep, she had. He'd taken all the care in the world; two tiny drops in a cup of black coffee, and she'd literally stopped talking in mid-sentence, leaned back in the chair, closed her eyes and, temporarily, stepped aside from a worry which was ripping her soul to shreds.

He looked down at her and smiled the concern of a man truly in love for the first time in his life. He saw the relaxed face; the slightly open mouth and the hint of spittle which accompanied each soft snore.

He murmured, 'It's for the best, sweetheart. He's not having you . . . what the hell it costs, he's not having you.'

Finney and Holmes were the only two people in the Billiard Room of Bordfield's fancy nick. Billiards and snooker are, primarily, winter games and the o'clock was such that even the all-year enthusiasts were at their homes for a meal, prior to a Saturday evening with their families or girl friends.

Holmes was annoyed at having been called out (and without explanation) by Finney, but he kept his annoyance strictly under wraps. He sat on a wall-bench, smoked a cigarette and, wherever he could, slipped a dampening remark upon Finney's furious enthusiasm.

Finney couldn't keep still. He prowled around the table, slamming the snooker-set 'blue' across the green cloth, and thumping and bouncing from the cushioned edge of the playing surface.

'How?' asked Holmes.

'Charterhouse. Page.' Finney grunted the two names in a tight, throw-away voice. 'How isn't important.'

'Meaning Charterhouse is in with him?'

'It's not impossible.'

'Oh, come *on*!'

'All right. If not Charterhouse, Page.'

'Why Page?'

'Because he's a two-timing, slimy bastard.'

'To tip us off . . . then tell *him* he's tipped us off?'

'Why not?' The blue snooker ball rebounded from a trio of cushions before disappearing into the top, right-hand pocket. Finney stooped and picked a 'red' from the rack under the pocket by his right thigh.

Holmes said, 'It doesn't make too much sense.'

'Germs like Page don't *have* much sense.'

'But there's always a reason . . . some sort of reason,' argued Holmes. 'If Page, *why* Page?'

Finney slammed the red ball up the table towards the top cushion, and growled, 'Could be, because he lost his job.'

'Eh?'

'I had a word with the head gardener, before we left.'

'A—er—"word"?'

'Don't go goody-goody on me, sergeant.'

'I'm interested,' said Holmes, coldly.

'He has sticky fingers,' snapped Finney, as he caught the red on a rebound, then sent it thudding round the cushion angles.

'*Had* sticky fingers,' corrected Holmes.

'Had—*has* . . . they never change.'

'God Almighty!'

'It isn't important.'

'The hell it isn't important. You smack a man around. You scare him into naming names. Then, you drop poison in the ear of a man you know damn well *must* make two and two come to six.'

'How do you know what I said?'

'I know *you* . . . Chief Inspector Finney.'

Finney turned and leaned on stiffened arms, with his back to the billiard table.

He rasped, 'Get your arse out of the sunshine, sergeant. These bastards are the germs we're expected to exterminate. All of 'em. And, any way we can.'

'By driving a man with a good job back to crime?' sneered Holmes.

'Could be, he still has that "good job".'

'But, not if *you* can help it.'

'Who's side?' said Finney, softly. Dangerously. 'Just who the hell's side are you on?'

'You know damn well . . .'

'That I don't. It's why I'm asking. Because, if you're on *their* side—if there's even a hint that your thinking runs along *their* lines—God help you, Holmes. I'll personally flesh you, all the way down to the bone.'

'I'm on your side,' growled Holmes, disgustedly. 'Some of your methods . . . they make me puke a little. But—and you know it—I'm on your side.'

'I'm obliged, sergeant,' sneered Finney. 'It needed verification . . . that's all.'

'Okay, now you've "verified".' Contempt met contempt, head-on. 'Now, get *your* arse out of the cesspit, and let's concentrate on bobbying.'

'With witnesses . . .' began Finney.

'I wouldn't have said that,' Holmes ended the remark. 'Nor would you have opened your mouth quite as wide. We're both gagged, when there's witnesses around. By a pension . . . not by the difference in rank. We both know it. There's not a cartload we can do about it. Either of us. A suggestion . . . from

137

a mere sergeant, of course. Let's sink our differences, and concentrate on nailing this father-in-law of yours.'

'I bet you enjoyed that little speech . . . eh?' said Finney,
tightly.

'It needed saying.'

'Especially the last bit? The "father-in-law" bit?'

'No.' Holmes squashed his cigarette into the lino of the
Billiard Room with the sole of a shoe. He shook his head, and
said, 'I didn't enjoy any of it. The pity is it had to be said.'

They stared at each other for a few seconds then, gradually,
the fury died in Finney's expression and was replaced by a
twisted smile.

'Okay,' he said. 'How he knows isn't important. That he
does know . . . that's all that matters. And *we* know he knows.
But, *he* doesn't know *we* know . . . and that gives us the edge.'

'Involved,' murmured Holmes.

'No. One jump ahead of the bastard . . . that's all that
matters.'

'You're going to be there?' asked Holmes.

'Naturally.'

'And you think Scarfe'll be there?'

'What else?' Finney frowned non-understanding. 'That's
what this goofball meet-me-on-the-canal-bank message was
sent for.'

'Ah! But, not from Scarfe . . . at least, not *openly* from
Scarfe.'

'For Christ's sake. He doesn't want his daughter to know.'

'Could be.' Holmes didn't sound fully convinced. He said,
'Okay—if you're right . . . why the meeting?'

'They're all tarred with the same bloody brush.' Finney
grinned, sardonically. 'He's fishing for a deal.'

'Dangerous,' mused Holmes. 'It means coming into the
open.'

'No-o. Double-talk . . . until he's sure.'

'But *then*, coming into the open.'

'When he's sure,' agreed Finney.

'Will he be sure?' asked Holmes.

'Oh, yes. Very sure . . . *I'll* see to that.'

'Sweetness and light,' smiled Holmes. 'And police corruption.'

'Complete with miniature mike, pocket transmitter . . . and half a dozen picked men hidden in the allotments.'

'But, of course.'

'Pick 'em well, sergeant. We're after big game. Aldermen, no less.'

5.45 p.m. . . .

In Leeds, the rains eased but, already, it had washed the few stains of blood from the smooth surface of the plastic mac.

The man turned into the main entrance of City Station, sought the toilets and, behind a locked door, eliminated the last traces of his clash with Conboy. He used toilet paper, soaked from the flush, to clean his hands and the smears of blood from the revolver. He took the knife from its sheath and, again using the flush, washed the crimson from the blade before drying it with more toilet paper.

He examined the revolver. It was a .38 calibre Smith & Wesson; a 'Centennial', five-shot with a snub-nosed 2″ barrel and a smooth, walnut stock. A pocket-sized man-stopper . . . a pocket-sized man-*killer*. And fully loaded.

Illegal . . . but, of course. Conboy could never have conned a Firearm Certificate from any police force in the U.K. Not with *his* record of violence. Maybe the gun had already killed; it wasn't beyond the bounds of possibility. The man shrugged at the thought. It didn't matter. It was going to kill again . . . after that, who cared?

Odd. He'd have paid clean money for the gun. He'd have happily paid over the odds . . . it was why he'd withdrawn money from the bank. And, moreover, the gun was perfect for his purpose. Small, but deadly.

Odd . . . how, at moments like this, Old Nick seemed to take 'fate by the scruff of the neck and make the near-impossible absurdly easy.

The man slipped the revolver into the side pocket of his jacket, buttoned the mac and walked from the toilets. He checked the time of the next train to Bordfield, then found the Refreshment Room and sat down at a table, with a cup of buffet tea and a cigarette, to wait.

And, on the outskirts of Bordfield . . .

Every city has its handful of similar houses. Victoriana enthusiasts go ga-ga about them; about the steep-sloped roofs and the multiplicity of ornate gable-ends; about the high, narrow windows and the porched doors. They are 'freehold' establishments, usually inhabited by mild eccentrics who refuse to be budged by anything short of a private Act of Parliament and the local authority—rather than spend time and money battling against sheer bloody-mindedness—by-pass them, and continue their sprawl of ticky-tack, leaving an oasis of olde worlde monstrosity at which passers-by might gawp.

This was one such place. It stood in its own couple of acres of knee-high weeds and had been (and still was) the birth-place of some of the most highly-prized cats ever to show a snooty, ramrod-straight tail to mere man.

'I think Princess Rhema of The Don,' mused Mrs. Lennox.

'Poor little bugger,' muttered Lennox, through a mouthful of food.

'What's that?'

'I dunno, though.' Lennox cleared his mouth, by swigging half the contents of a pint mug of hot, sweet tea. 'At least she might get good grub.'

'My darlings are all fed *scientifically*,' snapped Mrs. Lennox.

'That include me?' queried Lennox, drily.

They made the perfect couple. Each an animated butterball. Each, on the surface, not giving a damn about the feelings of the other . . . but, secretly, each counting the other as the finest person alive.

Only God, in His wisdom, knew why any woman could fall in love with a man like Lennox—or, come to that, why any man could fall in love with a woman like Lennox's wife—but it had happened, and it had worked . . . and the chemistry of mutual affection, although kept well hidden, was complete and forever.

Mrs. Lennox eyed her husband coldly, and said, 'What you're eating is good food.'

'Is it?' Lennox sounded to have his doubts.

'Balanced.'

'Oh, aye?'

'Full of vitamins. Full of proteins.'

'And bloody tasteless. What the hell is it? Shredded cardboard?'

'If you must smother it with sugar.'

'Sugar,' explained Lennox, 'is there to give it taste . . . and it's the only damn thing I *can* taste.'

'If you will smoke that disgusting pipe . . .'

'Not when I'm eating. Good God, I don't . . .'

'It destroys your taste buds . . .'

'Of all the codswallop . . .'

'Therefore good food is wasted on you.'

'Which,' grunted Lennox, 'is why you shove this glorified pap in front of me . . . that it?'

'I won't argue.' Mrs. Lennox drew herself up to her full, pouter-pigeon five-foot-five height. 'I will not argue with a complete oaf.'

Lennox nodded, and said, 'I don't blame you, lass. Neither would I.'

'We were talking about the kittens. Which Alderman Scarfe might prefer.'

'It's your show, pet.'

'Princess Rhema of The Don, Grand Duchess Sherbah of The Don or Prince Alex of The Don. One of those three, I think.'

Lennox chuckled, and said, 'Don't forget to mention . . . the "Don" you're talking about is the one that runs through Doncaster.'

'They are pure-blooded Russian Blues . . . as well you know.'

'Pure blooded,' agreed Lennox, amiably.

'Therefore . . .'

'They make you and me look like mongrels.'

'Speak for yourself, please.'

'Who else.' Lennox pushed himself away from the table and stood up. He said, 'He's your customer, old pet. I'll not be here.'

'Why not?'

'Reasons.' He waddled to the window and surveyed the sky. 'If the rain keeps off, I might have an hour or so playing bowls.'

'He's not coming until nine o'clock. No! . . . half-past. Probably later than that. He was very . . .'

'Then, onto the station to see everything's running smoothly,' rumbled Lennox.

'You'll be back . . . surely.'

'No, old pet.' Lennox turned and rubbed the nape of his thick neck as he said, 'Y'see, Alderman Scarfe . . . he ain't exactly my cup o' tea. I have this feeling. Like you, with cats. You sorta *know* . . . almost before they open their eyes. Me, too. Only, with me it's more of a pong . . . a nasty smell you might say.'

'You mean he's unclean? That he doesn't wash? An *alderman*?'

'No. Not quite that sorta muck.' Lennox grinned. 'But make him pay, pet. Thirty quid . . . not a penny less.'

'You need have no fear. He'll . . .'

''Cos I have this queer feeling. That he don't really *like* cats.'

('*A lot o' talk,*' *observed Lennox, cheerfully.*

'*I* want *to talk. I feel like talking.*'

The air was thick with cigarette and tobacco smoke. The seconds of the 'small hours' ticked their way towards the dawn of the Sabbath. The spools of the recorder turned, and the tape recorded every word.

There was also friendliness. Near-comradeship. It was as if Number Three Interview Room had, in some myterious way, transformed itself into the inner sanctum of a very select club; a place in which to exchange secrets and confidences.

But, the spools still turned, and the tape recorded every word.

Lennox said, 'All right, old son. You want to talk. I'm pre-pared to listen.'

'*Prison.*'

'*A subject you seem to favour . . . wouldn't you say?*'

'*I spent the first eight months in, and out, of prison hospital. In pain. Being patched up. The medics—they are good medics . . . but they were men. Like the inmates, they treated me like a moral leper.*'

'*The governor?*' *murmured Lennox*

'*You learn fast, in prison. You don't run to the "authorities" when you're hurt. When you're hounded. When you're victi-mised. If you do, you're going to be hurt again . . . even worse. No. You look around for a "protector". One of the block bosses. You play lackey to him. Fawn on him. Let him black-*

mail you. Anything! And, if he's big enough, you've bought yourself peace.'

'It's a hell of a price,' observed Lennox

'It's paid. Every day. Willingly.' There was a sigh-filled pause. 'I wouldn't pay it. The truth is, I couldn't pay it . . . one part of it. I couldn't force myself to turn "queer". That was the price—part of the price—and, I couldn't bring myself to pay it. Don't get me wrong. The code—the code, behind the wall—insisted that it was a not excessive price. A punishment-fit-the-crime price, in fact. A price applicable— fit and proper—to a child-rapist. But, I couldn't bring myself to pay it.'

'So?'

'I didn't have a "protector".' The ghost smile was sad and bitter. 'I was their—er—plaything. And they played very rough games—very rough games . . . and I spent most of that first year in hospital.')

6.30 p.m. . . .

The evening pulled its cloak of lengthening shadows closer around its shoulders, and prepared for nightfall. The thick cloud-cover created a false dusk and, in the shop, it was almost dark.

Scarfe didn't use the lights. From long usage, he knew the exact position of every counter and display cabinet. He locked the front door, then walked quietly to the strong-room. The empty Omo carton he carried looked incongruous in this emporium of comparative wealth.

Within ten minutes the carton was two-thirds filled with pieces taken from the safe, of which only Scarfe held a key. Silver cups and tankards; necklaces and bracelets; candlesticks and salvers. More than two score pieces . . . and every piece included on various lists of 'Stolen Property' circulated to the surrounding police forces. The weight was such that the corrugated cardboard of the carton threatened to twist and split, unless it was carefully handled.

Scarfe handled it *very* carefully.

He left the shop by the rear entrance and placed the carton alongside the wooden door leading to the yard at the back of the premises. Then, he returned to the shop, locked the rear entrance and left the shop by the front door.

Scarfe was sure nobody was watching, but Scarfe was a meticulously careful man. *Had* anybody been watching, what would they have seen? The owner of the shop, visiting his premises—probably to check that all the doors and safes were secured for the weekend—then leaving it, via the same door he'd used to enter. He'd entered empty-handed. He'd come out empty-handed. Jewellers the world over take similar elementary precautions.

He drove his car for more than ten minutes; twisting, turning, doubling back on his route and always keeping a keen eye on the driving mirror.

He was *not* being followed . . . he'd have wagered his life on that fact.

He turned into the narrow back street which paralleled the front of the shop, braked by the gate leading to the yard, unlocked the boot of his car and, within minutes, had the Omo carton locked away and speeding towards a safer hiding place, beyond Bordfield.

7 p.m. . . .

The man paid the driver, at the mouth of Raymon Crescent, gave a good tip, was thanked and watched the taxi do a smart U-turn before gathering speed, back towards Bordfield Railway Station.

The man took a deep breath, squared his shoulders a fraction, then began to walk along the half-circle of well-built, semi-detached houses. Each house was slightly different from its neighbour; even the two linked by a single dividing wall were never *quite* identical. Permutations were those of French windows and bay windows; porched entrances or unporched entrances; glass-fronted doors or mock-tudor doors; wrought-iron gates, or wooden gates. Tiny differences. Insignificant differences. But, nevertheless, the differences which made each house 'individual' and, therefore, not one of 'an estate'.

This was 'Jones's Land'—the kingdom of one-up-man-ship gone mad—where petty snobbery was hidden under the mis-use of the word 'pride'.

Each house was its owners personal 'castle', with battle-ments of privet hedges, vying with each other for height, thickness and angularity of cut. There was nothing pleasant about Raymon Crescent. It was clean. It held no litter. Its lamp-standards were all upright and unbroken. It was as surgically pure as an operating theatre . . . but, like an operat-ing theatre, it was not a pleasant place.

The man felt this, as he walked the even pavement. He felt the atmosphere of this small, self-important crescent of houses. An atmosphere of puny hatreds and minor jealousies; of polite back-biting and genteel indiscretions. Wife-swapping—in so far as wife-swapping was still a popular parlour game, and had not yet gone completely out of vogue—was still secretly practised in Raymon Crescent . . . and even *that* fact was felt, and realised, by a stranger capable of absorbing the overall 'atmosphere' of a district so immersed in itself as Raymon Crescent.

The man felt it, and the bitter-sad whisper of a smile touched his lips. He turned in at 'White Gates', walked up the drive and thumbed the bell-push.

Myra Finney answered the ring.

'Mrs. Finney?' he asked.

'Yes.' She nodded, then frowned and said, 'Don't I . . .'

'Know me?' The spectre-smile came and went. 'Yes, you do ... indeed, you do.'

'You're ...'

'Twelve years older. Twelve years dead.' He was past her, and into the hall. With one hand he closed the door. With the other hand he brought the revolver from his jacket pocket. He murmured, 'Who else is in the house?'

'Nobody—er—nobody ...' Her eyes fastened on the gun, as if hypnotised by its snub-nosed deadliness. 'Just—just me.'

'Your husband?'

'He's—he's out. On duty.'

'Children? Have you any children?'

'Three ... but they're not at home.'

'Where?'

'With their grandparents. They're with their grandparents for the weekend.'

'Dogs?'

'No. We don't ...' She shook her head, still staring at the gun. 'We don't have a dog.'

'Nice.' His voice was feather-soft. Frighteningly soft. He moved the snout of the gun, and said, 'We'll go inside, shall we? And, please don't scream. No fuss ... I want the minimum of fuss.'

Less than half a dozen steps down the hall, he saw the telephone on its mock-antique table.

He said, 'Stop!'

She froze.

'Something we don't need,' he said gently.

He lifted the handset from its rest and, holding it in his right hand, with the gun, he unscrewed the bakelite ear- and mouth-pieces, dropped them onto the carpet and cracked them with the heel of a shoe. Then he removed the slim, metal diaphragms, slipped them into his pocket and returned the useless handset to its rest.

'After you, Myra,' he said, softly.

Myra Finney nodded, dumbly, and led the way into the living room.

The man thought ...

She isn't afraid of me. She's startled. The gun worries her a little. She's ... perturbed. That's the word. 'Perturbed'. But, no more than that. As if an old illness, to which there is a cure, has suddenly recurred.

The man said, 'You're not frightened.'

'The gun scares me.' Her gaze remained fixed upon the revolver. 'If you took your finger away from the trigger, I'd feel safer. Happier.'

'I'm not here to make you happy. I don't want you to feel safe.'

They sat opposite each other, in armchairs. She was wearing bell-bottomed slacks, which tapered to skin-tightness around her hips; a silk blouse, tucked into the waist-band of the trousers; mules on her feet. The stretch of the blouse and slacks left no room for doubt; she was naked, underneath.

He still wore the plastic mac. Open, and draping to touch the carpet alongside the chair by his shoes. He held the Smith & Wesson easily—almost lightly—with its weight resting on his right thigh, and its snout aimed across the few feet which separated them. His finger was through the trigger-guard, and touching the trigger.

He said, 'Don't watch the gun, Myra. Watch me.'

She continued the stare at the revolver.

'I'm the one you harmed,' he said, softly. 'I'm the one who's returned ... not the gun.'

'I should warn you.' She swallowed, then continued, 'My husband's a ...'

'Detective chief inspector.' He ended the sentence for her. 'I know ... but not for long.'

148

For the first time, she dragged her gaze from the gun, and looked at his face.

'Ralph, too?' She asked the question in a dead, emotionless voice.

He nodded at her mouth; at the slightly swollen lip, half-hidden under the heavy lipstick.

'Ralph?' he asked.

'It hasn't been too easy,' she said, quietly.

'I think you deserved each other. Most people do.'

Her eyes clouded a little. They took on a dreamy, might-have-been expression; the expression of the teenager, when confronted by her current idol.

She murmured, 'Funny, isn't it? It might have been you.'

'Come *on*. I was a married man. Happily married.'

'It still might have been you,' she insisted, softly.

The man thought ...
Damn her, she's right. She could have. Played a certain way, *she could have!* *For all the wrong reasons. For all the shameful reasons. But, it's her I've thought about—dreamed about— remembered ... for twelve years. She knew it then. She still knows it. Of all the women I've ever known ...*

He said, 'You're kidding yourself.'

'Am I?' The question called him a liar. The coy, mocking smile which accompanied the question also called him a liar.

'Where's your husband?' he asked.

'On duty. I've already ...'

'Where?'

'God knows.' She shrugged. She seemed to have forgotten the revolver. 'We don't share secrets. There isn't much we *do* share.'

'Perjury?' he suggested, softly.

'I was only a kid, at the time ... remember?'

149

'It means I'll have to wait,' he sighed.

'What?'

'If you don't know where he is.'

'Oh?' She hesitated, then said, 'The canal bank. He's going to be there. There's some old allotments. He's going to be there, at ten o'clock.'

'You seem very sure.'

'It's to do with his job. Stolen property . . . something.'

'He told you this?'

'No . . . I told *him*. A tip-off. It came from my father. I passed it on.'

'So-o.' The ghost-smile appeared and vanished. 'From—what is it?—*Alderman* Scarfe . . . it has to be authentic.'

'That's where you'll find Ralph,' she said.

He closed his fingers more tightly around the butt of the revolver, raised it from its resting place on his thigh, pointed it at her middle and thumbed back the hammer.

'But,' he said, 'first you.'

(*'Then, what?' asked Lennox, flatly.*

The spools turned, and every word of the talk in Number Three Interview Room was recorded.

'She was scared. Terrified. For the first time in her life, I'd say.'

'You'd be scared,' growled Lennox. 'Some lunatic busts into your home, points a gun at you and is just gonna shoot you . . . you'd be scared.'

'No.' The denial carried absolute conviction. 'She gabbled a little. A certain amount of pleading. Some half-baked "explanation". That she was a kid, at the time. That she knew Finney. That the uniform had some sort of glamour . . . that sort of talk. That they fancied each other, and that the perjury had been Finney's idea. It probably was. But, I don't think she took too much persuading. Knowing her. Knowing the sort of

person she was . . . still is.'

'The gun?' asked Lennox, pointedly. 'The knife?'

'Do you think I'd walk into a police station, tell this story . . . and bring the knife and gun with me?')

The crown green was moist and lush, underfoot, after the recent rain. The excellent drainage prevented any sogginess and, already, two doubles were in progress. Lennox dropped the mat and one of the woods onto the turf, weighed the jack in his right hand and waited for his partner.

He glanced approvingly at the mass of colour in the border, beyond the tarmac path surrounding the bowling green, nodded his pleasure and said, ' A nice show this year, Mr. Page. Keep up the good work.'

Page grunted an unintelligible reply.

Page had nursed his grievance all day. His hatred for Finney had expanded to include Holmes and, from Holmes, via the illogicalities of anger and disgust, to envelope even Scarfe. Page hated the world . . . a world which (or so it seemed) refused the right of a man to let his past die, and be forgotten. The head gardener. His wife. Everybody! He was the proverbial dog with the everlasting bad name and, for the rest of his life, the world was going to kick him in the guts whenever it could.

Okay . . . he, too, could do some kicking.

He'd left the house to walk his simmering rage into some sort of control and, almost automatically, his feet had carried him to one of the parks. To one of the bowling greens.

And here was Lennox—another bloody copper—but, somehow . . .

'Had an accident, old son?' asked Lennox.

'Eh?'

'Your mouth. It looks as if you've hit it with something.'

'Finney did it,' muttered Page. Much of the anger turned

into a feeling of self-pity; all except one hard ball of hatred reserved for a certain detective chief inspector. He said, 'He needs taking in hand, Mr. Lennox. He's too handy with his fists.'

'*Our* Finney?' Lennox dropped the jack and second wood onto the turf, alongside the mat. In a very sombre voice, he said, 'Has he been fisting you?'

'It didn't oughta be allowed, Mr. Lennox.'

'It *isn't* allowed, old son.'

'Aye—well . . . somebody should tell *him*.'

Lennox said, 'Let's start the ball rolling by you telling me.'

Lennox didn't play bowls that evening. He apologised to his partner and, instead, sat alongside Page, in a secluded corner of the bowling green surround, listened and asked questions. Page talked. He talked for almost an hour. He exaggerated a little . . . but not much. He answered questions, and volunteered information which Lennox mentally accepted as being at least eighty-per-cent true. It was Page's 'finest hour'; the hour when all the pigeons of past affronts and almost-forgotten hurts limped home to roost. Self-pity and bitterness were like the surgeons' knives; they ripped Page wide open, and all the guts spilled out for Lennox to see and scowl at.

As they sat there, there was a temporary break in the clouds; the sun slanted its rays, and painted elongated shadows across the smooth turf, and it was a beautiful evening . . . for some.

8 p.m. . . .

Tim Chambers answered the door, and looked at the man with a puzzled expression. He had this feeling . . . that he knew the man, but couldn't place him. Some party, perhaps. Some potential customer he'd seen before.

The man said, 'Mr. Chambers?'

'Ye-es.' Chambers nodded, slowly, and continued to look

at the man's face while he rooted around in his memory.

'Can you spare me a few minutes?' asked the man.

'It depends.'

'It's important,' said the man, persuasively.

'To who? You? Or, me?'

'Both of us.'

Chambers said, 'I don't need my soul saving, if that's . . .'

'No' I'm not hawking religious tracts.' The ghost-smile flickered on and off. 'Nor encyclopaedias.'

The man thought . . .

A careful man. He demands to know how firm the ground is, before he takes another step forward. Therefore, a reliable man. Not a gambler. Not a fool. A man I might once have been proud to call 'friend'.

The man said, 'My wife.' He spoke softly, and looked at the face of Tim Chambers as he spoke.

'Oh!'

Near-recognition flirted with Chambers' expression.

'May I come in?' asked the man, politely.

Chambers hesitated, then said, 'Why not? It's an important subject. I think we should discuss it.'

'As civilised men,' murmured the man.

'Perhaps,' said Chambers, gently. As he stood aside, to let the man enter, he repeated, 'Perhaps.'

There was no more talk until they reached the main room of the apartment. Chambers waved a hand towards one of the leather wing-chairs, and the man nodded his thanks and sat down. Chambers walked to the tiny drinks cabinet.

He said, 'Civilised men . . . that's what you suggested. What would you like to drink?'

'Whisky, please. Fifty-fifty . . . whisky and water.'

153

'Ice?'

'No, thank you.'

The man thought . . .

I don't stammer any more. Yesterday—this morning—it was a real effort to speak. For years . . . but, now, I don't stammer any more. I must be growing accustomed to freedom. Or, is it the other thing? That everything I planned is happening? Something. Whatever it is, I don't stammer any more.

Chambers handed him his drink, then settled into the twin of the leather wing-chair. They stared at each other for a moment, then Chambers raised his glass.

'To civilised men,' he murmured.

The man said, 'To my wife.'

They each sipped from their glasses, and watched each other over the brim.

'You're different,' said Chambers.

'Really?'

'I've seen your photograph . . . a few times. That's why I almost recognised you, at the door.'

The man said, 'I wouldn't have thought.'

'What?'

'That she'd keep photographs of me.'

'A few. Snapshots, mostly.'

'It must have been embarrassing,' said the man. 'For you, I mean.'

'No,' Chambers shook his head.

'Really?'

'She's human. We all make mistakes.'

'By keeping the photographs?'

'By marrying you, in the first place.'

The man eyed Chambers carefully, for a moment, then said, 'And yet, you don't hate me.'

154

'I despise you,' said Chambers, calmly. 'Frankly, you're not important enough to hate.'

'Oh, yes . . . important,' contradicted the man, gently. 'Important enough to stand between you and my wife.'

'If you *can*.'

The man sipped his drink, then said, 'I hold the marriage certificate, Chambers.'

'A scrap of paper.'

'A very *important* scrap of paper.'

'It doesn't prove love.'

'No-o,' admitted the man, slowly. 'But—tell me . . . can *you* prove love?'

Now Chambers sipped his drink, before saying, 'I don't need it certifying. You have the piece of paper . . . but I have the woman.'

'Until I claim her.'

'You have no claim on her.' Chambers' tone was brittle.

'Conjugal rights?' mocked the man.

Chambers breathed, 'You're a bastard. You'd even do *that*.'

'The law put me behind bars,' said the man.

'For a particularly foul rape.'

'I can now use that same law.'

'For *legal* rape.'

The man nodded, slowly.

Chambers snapped, 'What the hell sort of an animal are you?'

The man thought . . .

It was going to be so 'civilised'. And this, already. This man doesn't anger readily. He isn't the sort. He hates slowly but, when hatred comes it stays. Forever. Presumably the same with love. A solid man. A man who, however great the temptation, would never commit rape . . . would never be treacherous. Or, would he?

155

The man held the whisky in his left hand. With his right hand, he pulled the Smith & Wesson from his jacket pocket, cocked the hammer, hooked a finger around the trigger and levelled it at Chambers.

In a cold, business-like voice, he said, 'Keep away from my wife, Chambers.'

For a moment Chambers looked surprised. Not afraid, but surprised to a degree which almost amounted to shock.

Then, he said, 'Or, what?'

'This.' The man moved the revolver, menacingly.

'Don't be a fool. You wouldn't dare.'

The man said, 'I've been in bad company, Chambers. For the last twelve years, I've lived with some very dangerous men. It makes a difference. You name it . . . I *dare*.'

'You—you're bloody *primitive* !' gasped Chambers.

'Hang on to that belief. It may save your life.'

Chambers tasted his whisky, to gain time, then said, 'You're really out of your mind, y'know. You can't be with her twenty-four hours a day. You can't keep her locked away. That damn gun isn't going to help.'

'I'll hear things,' the man assured him.

'And, if you do?'

'You'd better find a lot of corners to duck behind. I'll come looking.'

'To *kill* me?'

In a flat, emotionless tone, the man said, 'I can rape. I can kill. The gap between the two isn't very wide.'

'You're crazy.'

'That's not impossible,' agreed the man. He creased his forehead in thought for a moment, then said, 'We could save time. and trouble. It's up to you, Chambers.'

'How?'

'You're an honourable man . . . wouldn't you say?'

'What the hell do you know about . . .'

156

'We're talking about *you*, Chambers.'

'We're talking in riddles.'

'No. We're talking about my wife . . . and you.'

Chambers waited.

The man said, 'I want your solemn promise. Now!'

'At the point of a gun?' sneered Chambers.

'That. Or I end the slap-and-tickle . . . permanently.'

'Go to hell.'

'Your promise,' insisted the man, coldly. 'That you won't see my wife again. Otherwise.'

'You'll shoot me?'

The man nodded, slowly. Very convincingly.

'You'll kill me?'

Again, the man nodded, hooked a thumb over the hammer of the revolver and put full pressure on the trigger. Tim Chambers was within the weight of a coin from sudden and violent death.

'You *mean* it?' It was a last verification.

The man said, 'I mean it.'

Tim Chambers tasted his whisky, to moisten his lips then, very deliberately, said, 'Go ahead and shoot, madman. I don't doubt you will. I don't doubt you even *want* to. As you say— rapist, murderer . . . there's not a lot of difference. It's the only way you'll stop me. I happen to love your wife . . . something you wouldn't understand. With, or without, a divorce—with, or without, your approval—I'm going to see her again. Often. As often as possible. That piece of paper— that marriage certificate—it means damn-all. We're man and wife . . . *we* are. In our own eyes. And that's all that matters. So-o, if that's your crazy answer, go ahead. It's the only way you'll stop me. But, it'll also stop *you* . . . this time you'll be put out of her life for a lot longer than twelve years.'

('*That gun*,' *rumbled Lennox.* '*You've used it a lot, today.*'

'*Justifiably.*'

'*By your yardstick.*'

'*The gun was better than the knife. Less crude.*'

'*I doubt,*' said Lennox, '*whether you'd have used the knife.*'

The spools turned. The tape recorded the conversation. Neither of the men were now smoking, but the scarves of tobacco smoke draped the upper air of Number Three Interview Room, and seemed to create a world slightly to one side of the world of reality.

The room was an entity, to itself. The two occupants were like castaways on a desert island; they were there and, whether or not they liked each other, their situation demanded that they tolerate each other. Companionship, without friendship. Complete honesty, without particularly liking each other. Respect, but no comradeship.

The mixture was odd. A mixture peculiar to police interview rooms and, even then, only between certain types of men.

'*Knives,*' chuckled Lennox, '*are very nasty things.*'

'*Any nastier than guns?*'

'*No-o—but more personal . . . much more personal.*'

'*I'd have used the knife. Never think I wouldn't.*'

'*If you say so.*'

'*I was paying off very personal accounts.*'

'*Aye . . . there is that,*' agreed Lennox.

'*I'd have used the knife.*'

'*By the way,*' said Lennox, '*where is the knife?*'

'*With the gun.*'

*Lennox sighed, and said, '*Of course. It would be.*'*

The tape recorded a few seconds of silence.

*Lennox rubbed his chops, and said, '*I think it's high time, old son.*'*

'*What's that?*'

'*The Official Caution. You ain't been the complete sobersided citizen, y'know. At a rough estimate, I reckon you've*

smashed half the rules in the book . . . on your own admission.'
'I haven't finished, yet.'
*'No. But, before you tell the rest, I think the Official
Caution. A bit belated . . . but necessary.')*

8.30 p.m. . . .

There is a theory; that fat men are peculiarly nimble and
light-footed. Lennox wished to hell the theory held enough
water with which to wash a pair of socks because, as far as
he was concerned, it bloody-well *didn't.*

He was breathless, panting and wheezing and (so far) the
only thing he'd done was telephone; the heaviest thing he'd
lifted had been a telephone receiver.

To his wife . . .

To tell that mystified lady that she must note the very
second when Alderman Scarfe arrived to purchase his blue-
blooded pussy-cat. Then to engage him in as prolonged a conversation as possible—to give him tea and buns, if necessary—
but to pump him into telling her where he'd been, immediately
prior to his arrival. Had he come straight from his home?
Had he, perhaps, called in for a jar, en route? Who had he
seen? Who had he talked to?

'. . . Oh, and another thing. Don't sell him one of the
moggies. I don't give a damn if he offers a hundred quid a
whisker . . . *don't.* Kid him on—kid him on, as long as
possible—but I don't want to be connected to that crafty
boyo . . . not even via one of my wife's cats.'

To the Borfield C.I.D. Office . . .

To issue detailed instructions to a puzzled detective constable who was there to keep one of the chairs warm. To get
himself off to his (Lennox's) happy abode and there get himself tucked away in a dark corner, in the grounds of the house.
To wait for the arrival of Scarfe's car. To note the time of the

arrival. To note exactly how long Scarfe was inside the house. To check the milometer on Scarfe's car and make a note of the mileage.

'. . . Then, when he comes out, you grab his collar. The charge—if he gets stroppy—is suspicion of handling stolen property. Bring him back to the nick in his own car. I'll be waiting. Remember what he says . . . every word. But, don't be browbeaten, lad. He'll try it, but handle him like you'd handle any other tea-leaf. And, once he comes out of the house, don't let him near his car.'

To the home of Alderman Scarfe . . .

To express feined surprise for the benefit of the slightly bewildered Mrs. Scarfe.

'. . . Well, if he's not home, that's it then, isn't it, ma'am? I just wanted a quick word with him about summat? But if, as you say, you haven't seen him since about six, it'll have to wait. Not to worry, missus. It'll save. I'll probably see him tomorrow . . . if not before.'

To Bordfield Radio Room . . .

To the sergeant in charge of sending and receiving all messages passing along the air-waves. Again, with very detailed and specific instructions.

'. . . The number of Scarfe's car. The description. You know it. Okay, I want it passed to every squad car and every copper in, and around, Bordfield. As far afield as you like . . . but let 'em all know. I want it seen, by as many coppers as possible. Where, when, which direction it was taking, if it was parked, where it was parked. That sorta thing. I don't want it stopped. I don't want it tailed. I just want to be able to say exactly where it was—exactly what it was doing—as from this phone call.'

To the home of Detective Chief Inspector Finney . . .

No answer. He dialled a second time. Still no answer. He dialled the operator, and asked her to try. Still no answer . . .

not even the 'engaged tone'.

'It sounds as if it's been cut off, sir.'

'Has it hell been cut off,' snarled Lennox.

'There's no need to be nasty with me, sir. It's not my . . .'

'Sorry. I'm a bad-tempered old sod. I'm sorry.'

'I'll get the engineer round, as soon as possible, sir. It won't be till Monday, I'm afraid. But I'll get them round as soon as possible.'

'Aye . . . thanks.'

Back to Bordfield nick, and to the senior officer on duty . . .

A uniformed superintendent. A man to whom Lennox opened his heart, and showed his disgust.

'I'll be in, later this evening, Harry. Meanwhile, find Finney. Tell him—from me—that he's suspended from duty, pending enquiries. And, if he asks questions, tell him damn-all . . . that *I'll* tell him why, when I see him. He's out, somewhere. I think he's after Scarfe . . . for receiving. I don't give a monkey's. Finney is off duty, from the very second you contact him. He's a disgrace to the bloody force, and he's gonna be tamed.'

Back to the home of Detective Chief Inspector Finney . . .

Three times and, each time, he heard the 'number unobtainable' tone.

Lennox pulled a large handkerchief from his pocket and wiped the sweat from his forehead and from his multiple chins and neck.

As he lowered himself onto a seat in the bowling pavilion, he growled, 'Christ, They do it all the time on T.V. And they never snarl the bloody thing up like *this*.'

9 p.m. . . .

But Finney . . .

Finney, Holmes and a quartet of known 'leaners' from the

C.I.D. pool, were sorting themselves out in the darkness of weed-tangled allotments.

'How long,' grunted Finney, 'since some clown grew cabbages in this lot?'

'Eight years. Maybe ten,' said Holmes.

'So, why the hell don't the council . . .'

At which point Finney caught a foot in hidden chicken-wire and sprawled into the knee-high undergrowth.

There was a pause for pithy language. Holmes and the four muscle-boys waited patiently; they weren't shocked—they'd heard all the words before—and, anyway, it served Finney right for buggering up their Saturday night's planned revelry.

As he hauled himself upright, Finney spat his fury at Holmes.

He said, 'I ordered six. Why only four?'

'You asked for men who could handle themselves. Bully-boys, in other words.'

'I said *six.*'

'For one man? Eight of us?' mocked Holmes.

'I don't trust the bastard.'

'If he sports those sort of muscles . . .'

'Don't be funny, sergeant. You know what I mean.'

'No . . . I don't.'

One of the heavies growled, 'We can handle him, sir. Say the word. We'll break every bone in his body.'

'That, you won't!' snapped Holmes.

Finney dusted himself down, and said, 'I'll tell you if I need rough stuff . . .'

'At which point, I walk out,' said Holmes.

'. . . At which point,' sneered Finney, 'Sergeant Holmes goes home to watch The Flower Pot Men.'

'Just you tell us when, sir,' said the heavy.

Holmes checked his rising disgust, and said, 'We're after evidence. Not blood. You linked up, sir? That mike . . . is it functioning properly?'

'Naturally.' Finney made it sound as if the microphone hidden behind his tie wouldn't *dare* to malfunction.

'That's it, then.' Without appearing to do so, Holmes took over the ribbons of command. He said, 'You four. Space yourselves out. Get down in the weed . . . and keep your eyes on Mr. Finney. Keep those walkie-talkies switched on to "receive", and *listen*. If somebody meets Mr. Finney, I want a time check and every word remembered. Every word! Note where you are. Note where Mr. Finney is. Estimate the distance, and be able to say how clearly you can hear the conversation. You're going to be cross-examined . . . *hard*. Think of all the questions you're going to be asked, and make sure you have the answers ready.'

'Where are you going to be?' asked Finney, gruffly.

'There's a hut—an old garden-shed—up near the bridge. It's a bit broken-down, but it'll give enough cover. I'll be able to see, as well as hear.'

Finney said, 'You don't trust me too far, do you, sergeant?'

Holmes didn't answer.

Finney spoke to the other four men. He said, 'That's it, then. You know what to do. No talking. No smoking. No flashing of torches. You're not there, till you're needed. But, the minute I make the pinch, you come out in a hurry.'

'But,' warned Holmes, quietly, 'not *fighting*.'

Bordfield. Lessford. Twin cities (with Lessford fractionally the larger) but each a part of the same Metropolitan Police District. Each sharing the same chief constable and the same two deputy chief constables. A massive, unwieldy law-enforcement body . . . or, so the majority argued. Impersonal. Without a soul; incapable of the close-knit camaraderie so vital to the functioning of a razor-edge force . . . or, so the majority argued.

163

But, because of its very size, it had certain things going for it.

Example . . .

Lessford had its 'warehouse fringe'; a cluster of streets resembling brick-sided canyons. Streets broad enough to allow the easy passage of heavy vehicles, but streets with few windows and streets with heavy, wooden doors. Some of the warehouses were 'bonded', and this handful lacked even windows; where the windows had been were carefully 'locked-in' bricks, and the whole, rectangular building was like a piece from a giant's nursery play-blocks. Some of the warehouses were still in use; within their gloomy depths they stored everything from ping-pong balls to lawnmowers—from bottled sweets to box-mattresses; they were the reservoirs of the thousand and one bits and pieces of impedimenta necessary for the smooth running of 'civilisation'.

And, here and there, an empty warehouse; broken windowed, rat-infested and cobweb-curtained; great caves of dusty echoes, strong with the stench of damp and decay.

One of the empty warehouses wasn't as empty as it should have been.

Scarfe worked from the reflected glow of a moderately well-lit road. He used a length of discarded steel piping as a crow-bar and worked hard to loosen the last floorboard. The first few had been easy—half-rotten, and held in position with rusted nails . . . but (as usual) there was *always* one awkward bastard.

It came away, at last, and he dropped to his knees, struck a match and peered into the cavity beneath the floor-space. It was deep enough—maybe a bit too deep—but (the main thing) it was safe.

He hefted the Omo carton then, spreadeagling himself on the filthy flooring he lowered the carton and contents into the hole for the full length of his arms, then let go. He estimated a two foot drop, before the cardboard hit the rubble and the contents of the carton rattled like so much tin.

The Lessford patrol car made one of its thrice-nightly zigzags along the roads of 'warehouse-land'. The headlights caught the bonnet of the Jag, parked without lights, half-way along the cul-de-sac. For a split second the front number plate was readable.

The squad car observer said, 'It's there. Keep moving.'

'I saw it,' grunted the driver . . . and 'kept moving'.

The observer unhooked the hand-mike, pressed the transmit button and said, 'Bordfield Control. Bordfield Control. This is X-ray Fifty. We've spotted Scarfe's car.'

Lennox was still telephoning; this time from his own office, and on the internal line to Bordfield Radio Room.

He was saying, '. . . Great. They know where it is? . . . Tell 'em to stay clear for half an hour—at least half an hour—then do another run. We've already had him spotted making for Lessford. Now we know where in Lessford. You say it's alongside a disused warehouse? . . . Fine. Half an hour, then. Then, if the car's not there, have 'em radio in, and get the forensic boffins on the job. There'll be muck on his shoes, if he's been in the warehouse—maybe on his clothes—and I want a nice, fat comparison sample . . . Then I want the warehouse searched. Don't worry about search warrants. I'll fix things, and you can make that a direct order from me, in case of come-backs . . . Oh, and one more thing. There's a detective constable on his way to my house. Huggett—I think that's his name . . . he might even be there, by now. He'll be on radio. Tell him, from me, not to wait for Scarfe to go into the house . . . That's right, sergeant. *My* house. He wants to buy a kitten, if you *must* know. Tell Huggett—or whatever his name is—to nab him, the minute he arrives. Nab him, caution him and drag him back here. And, without the Jag . . . Oh, and just to smooth out the rough edges, tell everybody to keep their eyes skinned. I still want a progress report on Scarfe's car, if it's spotted coming back from Lessford.'

The man thought . . .
This is it, then. This is what you've been planning for all these years. Revenge. Vengeance. Maybe it's not quite as sweet as it's cracked out to be, but it's not sour. It has a nice, warm feel. It doesn't repay . . . nothing can ever repay. But it balances the scales a little. It makes damn sure you're not the only mug in the world.
   Two down, and one to go.
   And, the grandstand finish . . . the way all fights should end.

9.30 p.m. . . .

The man played it safe; everything had run silk-smooth, so far, and common caution insisted that, for it to continue so, all he needed was a little care. The plastic mac, for example; it was too cumbersome—it flapped around and hindered fast movements—therefore, he rid himself of the mac, rolled it into a tight parcel and crammed it into a half-empty litter-bin.

Coincidentally, and within seconds of him ridding himself of the mac, it started to rain again. Not like the previous downpour, but a gentle, summer's evening drizzle. It left the fast-darkening sky and floated, rather than fell, to earth.

He reached the canal bank, not via the steps leading down from Brent Bridge, but via a semi-secret route, known to himself from his youth; alongside the wall of a mill, over a fence, then down the slope of an embankment. He reached the towpath about half a mile upstream from Brent Bridge, and with the bridge between himself and the old allotments. It was safer, that way. He'd approach from an unexpected direction. He'd have the element of surprise on his side.

When he reached the gloom of the path, he unbuttoned his jacket, took the Smith & Wesson from his pocket and settled it into the waistband of his trousers.

He walked slowly. Eyes searching the gathering darkness ahead, and the banking leading down to the path. He moved from shadow to shadow; smoothly, and without haste. The hunter, concentrating all his attention upon the tracking down of his prey.

The uniformed superintendent frowned, and said, 'We don't know where, Lenny. We've tried his house . . . no answer.'

'Phoned?' asked Lennox.

The superintendent nodded, then said, 'There's a rumour. That he's taken Holmes and a handful of the rough lads from C.I.D., somewhere.'

'Where?'

'Nobody knows.'

'He's humped it too far, this time,' said Lennox, heavily. 'He's fisted Page . . . and Page is out for blood. *And*, I don't blame him.'

'For information?' asked the superintendent.

Lennox looked sad, and said, 'Aye . . . and he *got* the information. That's the part that's all wrong, Harry. Without a thumping, I doubt whether Page would have' opened up. But he *did* open up. Then, he opened up to me. All he'd told Finney . . . plus a complaint. We have what we wanted, but only because Finney did what he shouldn't do.'

'Bad,' murmured the superintendent.

'Good 'uns, bad 'uns . . . it takes all sorts.'

The telephone on Lennox's desk rang. The obese detective picked it up and grunted satisfactory replies.

He replaced the receiver, and said, 'One of the foot patrol constables. He's spotted Scarfe's car, on its way back to Bordfield.'

'Alderman Scarfe?' The superintendent raised surprised eyebrows.

'He's been taking all the nicked silverware, and such, we've been pestered with, lately . . . that's the strong suspicion.'

'Good God!'

'That's where Finney is . . . somewhere.'

'Where?'

'We-ell, wherever it is, he's astride the wrong horse. He ain't with Scarfe.' Lennox pushed himself free of the desk chair, and rumbled, 'C'mon. We'll nip along to Finney's house. See what the hell's wrong with the telephone.

The trio of strong-arms climbed from the Ford Cortina. The driver checked that all the doors were locked, and that the car was neatly parked where it was *allowed* to park and where it wouldn't attract attention.

Then, they walked, almost leisurely, toward Brent Bridge.

They were three of Conboy's 'soldiers'. Tough nuts whose profession concerned itself with the infliction of pain and (occasionally) the taking of life. They had no fear. They had no doubts. This was a straightforward smashing—maybe a homicidal smashing—but that didn't cause any of them undue concern. The alibis were already fixed; they could each 'prove' that they weren't together and that not one of them was within twenty miles of Bordfield.

They walked as a pair, followed by their companion. The two in front chatted inconsequentialities; the mild misery of the weather, how it might effect the 'going' at Monday's race meeting, and the nags which might, or might not, 'romp home'. Their talk was non-intellectual . . . but, come to that, so was their errand.

(*'I reckon,' mused Lennox, 'that you had premeditated murder buzzing around under your bonnet.'*

168

The tape recorded the remark, along with the rest of the conversation.

'Who knows what a man thinks?'

'The man?' suggested Lennox.

'Only while he's thinking it. By the time he gets to thinking it, the thought's already there.'

'That revolver was a mite more substantial than a thought, old son.'

'It was a revolver. The knife was a knife.' The voice was flat, and without life.

'Meaning a gun's nothing, until a man decides to pull the trigger? A knife's nothing, until a man decides to carve somebody's guts with it?'

'Something like that.'

Lennox growled, 'The argument leaks a bit, old son.'

There was a deep sigh, then the question, 'Do you know what a "Joey" is?'

'Criminal slang.'

'Conboy called me "Joey". That's not my name . . . but that's what he called me.'

'Aye . . . I noticed.'

'You know what it means?'

'I reckon.'

'In case you don't—in case you only half-know—I'll tell you . . .')

9.45 p.m. . . .

Other men would not have heard the sound. Even without the background hum of the city; without the muffled sound of distant traffic; without the faraway accompaniment of Bordfield, winding itself up to a crescendo of Saturday-night revelry. Even without these things, a man with normal hearing wouldn't have heard the sound.

But, these three were not normal men. They lived in a world of assault and pain which, in turn, meant that they lived on the edge of fear. Their coinage was agony, but the tit-for-tat maxim held good in their world, too. They were, therefore, ever on the look-out for men of their own kind; men who might, in turn, deliver agony to *them*.

Their eyes and ears were attuned to their way of life.

All three heard the oiled click of the revolver being cocked.

At first, they couldn't see the man. Nor could the man see them. He was flattened into the dark shadow of the bridge. He'd heard the footsteps of the men, descending the stone steps leading from the road to the towpath and he'd eased the revolver from his waistband and thumbed back the hammer . . . then, he'd heard the footsteps stop.

For a few seconds, he stood motionless. Waiting. Listening. Then, with infinite care, he eased aside the skirt of his jacket and drew the knife from its sheath, with his left hand. Then, once more, he waited.

The three men on the steps glanced at each other. They sent messages to each other, with their eyes. One of them nodded, then cat-footed back to the top of the steps, hurried across the road and silently descended the steps on the other side of the bridge. He paused at the bottom and, from his hip-pocket, took out a flick-knife. The blade shot from its housing, without a noise, and the pale backlash of the overhead street lighting was reflected upon the surface of honed steel.

The man waited, and listened. He flicked his eyes left, and right as he tensed himself for action. Animal instinct took over. Not sight, not hearing, not smell. The sixth sense which he'd developed over the last dozen years; the sense which had kept him free of much trouble; the sense which had steered him away from certain corners, away from certain landings, away from certain men.

He waited, and knew the high-rise of all his thought-out

plans was now, and within the next few minutes.

The uniformed superintendent braked the car in front of the house called 'White Gates'.

Lennox said, 'You stay here,' and had the car door open, and was heaving himself from the seat, almost before the car stopped.

He hurried up the path, gave a token jab at the bell-push, then opened the unlocked door and entered the house.

The uniformed superintendent waited.

There was something happening. Something big. Something which was worrying old Lenny . . . and Lennox wasn't the type to worry about many things. It had to do with Finney. It also had to do with Scarfe.

Less than ten minutes later, Lennox re-appeared. He almost ran to the car.

As he closed the door, he gasped, 'Brent Bridge . . . and step on it.' The car pulled away, and Lennox leaned over his stomach, picked up the hand-mike, and sent a message to the Radio Room.

'Chief Superintendent Lennox, here. Finney's place. I want a policewoman, two uniformed constables and a medic there, at the double. Nobody goes in, nobody comes out, without my say-so. I want the coppers on guard, front and rear.'

Finney stared into the surrounding gloom. The scum-covered surface of the canal was like a dust-surfaced mirror; it distorted the lights of the city, caught them and hazed them, but did little to reflect them. It was dark—too dark to see more than fifty yards, or so, along the towpath—and the slight curve of the path hid the steps of the bridge from view.

Finney didn't want Scarfe to have first sighting. It was a slight tactical advantage . . . to step out, and scare a little. Scarfe was a man against whom every trick had to be played to the full. To make him convict himself, out of his own mouth —to kid him on that a 'deal' was possible—was going to mean some fancy double-talk. Surprise . . . that was the first weapon. Therefore, Finney didn't want Scarfe to have first sighting.

Scarfe was being arrested.

The detective constable was a little dry-mouthed. After all, an *alderman*! You didn't feel an alderman's collar every day of the week. But—y'know . . . old Lenny was a great guy. You could trust him. If he said do a thing, you did it, knowing that the fat old slob would be right there, behind you, all the way to hell and back.

As Scarfe climbed from the Jag, the D.C. stepped forward and said, 'Alderman Scarfe? Alderman Frank Scarfe?'

'Ye-es.' Scarfe smiled, but answered very carefully.

The D.C. cleared his throat, then plunged in.

'Mr. Scarfe, sir. I have to tell you, you're under arrest . . .'

'What the hell!'

'. . . on suspicion of handling stolen property.'

Scarfe bluffed. He snarled, 'Don't talk like a damn fool. Who the devil are you, anyway?'

'Police. Detective Constable Huggett, sir. And, you're under arrest.'

'Don't be an idiot, Huggett.'

'You're not obliged to say anything, Mr. Scarfe. But, I have to warn you, whatever you say will be noted, and may be given in evidence.'

'Get out of my way, you young fool.'

Scarfe made as if to brush Huggett aside, like an annoying insect.

This was a very basic mistake, because Huggett was not an annoying insect . . . he was an increasingly *annoyed* detective constable. Like most men, he didn't enjoy being called a fool and an idiot.

172

He grabbed Scarfe's wrist, twisted and was in immediate control of the situation.

'Sorry, sir,' he lied, as he damn near broke Scarfe's wrist, 'but I have my orders. You're under arrest. You've been told why. You've been cautioned. Now—please, behave yourself... Detective Chief Superintendent Lennox wants to have a few words with you. *If* you don't mind.'

The man thought...
There's more than one, and they're not the police. The police don't do it this way. The police put their heads down and charge. When the cops come in, it's more like an elephantine stampede. Steamroller tactics.

But, not these boys.

These boys remind me of the animals I've been caged up with...

The attack came suddenly and silently, but the man was waiting for it.

The tearaway with the flick-knife came at him from his right, and the duo of fellow-bully-boys came in from his left. One of the pair had a blackjack already swinging. The other sported brass knuckles on both fists. They came in swiftly, and without noise.

The man side-stepped, estimated that the flick-knife might arrive first and swung the Smith & Wesson, tilted the muzzle downwards and fired a warning shot across his own body. The flick-knife boy swerved to a sudden halt as the slug dug dirt out of the towpath less than a yard from his feet.

The other two slowed slightly, but came on.

The blackjack merchant had his arm raised for the first wallop, as the man swept the blade of the sheath knife up, and across; the steel cut through cloth, skin and flesh and stopped

173

only when it touched bone. The blackjack boy screamed, dropped his weapon and backed off, nursing his maimed arm.

The impetus of the knuckle-duster expert carried him forward.

The man turned to meet him and rammed the short muzzle of the revolver into the soft part of his belly.

That stopped him . . . very suddenly.

'Back off!' snarled the man.

'Sure. Sure, I'll . . .'

The knuckle-duster boy backed away, at speed. He backed away a little too far. His foot slipped and, like some character from a B class comedy film, he toppled backwards into the slime of the canal.

That left the flick-knife boy, and the flick-knife boy did a quick calculation of the changed odds, and wasn't happy with the result. He hesitated, saw the Smith & Wesson arcing towards him, then turned and raced for the steps he'd just come down.

The man stood there, panting a little.

In the distance, from around the bend of the canal, he heard voices and the sound of men running. He tossed the sheath knife into the canal, then followed the flick-knife wallah towards the far steps.

10 p.m. . . .

The rain started up again, as the man straightened his jacket and hurried up the shallow steps leading to the main entrance of Bordfield Police H.Q.

At the public counter he was met by a smilingly polite constable.

The P.C. said, 'Yes, sir. Can I help you?'

'I'd like to see a senior officer,' said the man.

'About what, sir?'

'It's confidential, I'm afraid.'

'I'll need to know something, sir.' The P.C. glanced at his watch. 'It's a bit late. There isn't a senior officer around at the moment.'

'Get one,' said the man, wearily.

'It's not as easy as that, sir.'

'For God's sake!' The man looked bone tired, and not a little irritated. 'Get me a senior officer, constable. A detective, if possible. What I have to say is important.'

'What is it you *have* to say, sir?'

'Not to you, constable.'

The P.C. looked determined. Still polite, but adamant.

He said, 'I'm sorry, sir. If you'll just give me some inkling of what it's about.'

'It's *important*,' sighed the man.

'That's not enough, sir. That's too vague.'

The night-shift officers made their way past the man; behind him and out into the early darkness. They buttoned their macs against the midsummer rain as they neared the main entrance of the police station.

'Scarfe?'

Lennox loaded the question with make-believe surprise. His eyes rounded and his brows lifted as he play-acted astonishment for the benefit of the furious Finney.

'He was due to meet me here.' Finney almost shouted the words.

'Here?'

'On this towpath.'

'Scarfe?'

'For Christ's sake! I keep telling you . . .'

'Better get the blood-wagon, Harry.' Lennox spoke to the uniformed superintendent who'd driven him to Brent Bridge. He glanced at the tearaway with the badly slashed arm. 'And arrange for somebody to meet the ambulance at the hospital. His Nibs has a few questions to answer, after the knit-one-pearl-two treatment.'

'Will do.' The uniformed superintendent hurried up the steps, leading from the towpath to the road.

'And you.' Lennox eyed the tearaway who had just dragged himself from the canal. He raised his gaze and mused at the drizzle which was turning into a downpour, then said, 'You're wet, old son. But, we're *all* gonna be wet, if we stay here much longer.'

'Scarfe!' bawled Finney.

'Easy, Ralph,' warned Holmes, quietly.

'Aye . . . easy, *Ralph*.' Lennox echoed Holmes's words, but the warning differed from the warning murmured by Holmes. He stared at Finney for a second, then said, 'I think you'd better make for home, chief inspector.'

'Eh?'

'You, too, Sergeant Holmes.'

Finney blared, 'What the hell . . .'

'You're in trouble, Finney. Don't make things worse for yourself.' Lennox's voice was suddenly deep-frozen. 'Suspended from duty . . . that's the official terminology. You've used your fists once too often. You, too, Holmes. You stood by, and let it happen. I'll meet you in the chief's office, at ten o'clock, tomorrow morning . . . both of you.'

'Yes, sir,' sighed Holmes.

'Yes, sir, be damned! What the hell . . .'

'*Finney!*' Lennox shoved his multiple chin forward, aggressively.

'Ralph,' pleaded Holmes. 'For God's sake.'

Finney deflated. He'd heard rumours about this fat slob Lennox. Rumours which, at first glance—at first hearing—seemed outrageous. But, now they didn't . . . they didn't seem at all outrageous. Indeed, at that moment, he realised they

176

were not, after all, *rumours.*

He took a deep breath, blew out his cheeks, then grunted, 'Yes, sir. Tomorrow morning . . . ten o'clock, at the chief's office.'

Finney and Holmes passed the uniformed superintendent, as the uniformed superintendent hurried down the steps, and back to the towpath.

The quartet of muscle-conscious detective constables waited silently.

The uniformed superintendent said, 'Ambulance on its way, sir.'

'Good.' Lennox turned to the senior of the detective constables. 'You . . . take this soaked specimen back to the nick. A change of clothing—something from the stores—then bung him in a cell . . . after that, you're off duty. The rest of you. Hang around till the ambulance arrives, then one of you go with Sunny Jim to the needlework department—hand him over to whoever's there . . . then *you* go off duty. The other two . . . off duty, as soon as the ambulance arrives. And, all four of you . . . the chief's office, ten o'clock. They won't mean much, but have your excuses ready.'

The detective constables said, 'Yes, sir,' like a well-rehearsed barber's shop quartet.

Lennox surveyed them with open disgust.

He growled, 'The bish-bash-bosh brigade. All brawn. No brains. Off the record—I think you stink . . . all four of you.'

10.15 p.m. . . .

As the bell rang, the sergeant snapped, 'I'll take it,' and hurried away from the counter.

The P.C. looked uncomfortable, and said, 'Look, sir, we can't waste time . . .'

'You're not wasting time,' interrupted the man.

177

'We've other things to do. Important things.'

'*This* is important.'

The P.C. compressed his lips, reached a decision, then said, 'Okay. But you'll have to wait.'

'I'm quite prepared to wait.'

As he lifted the flap of the counter, the P.C. said, 'Come with me, please. Number Three Interview Room. It's just down the corridor. You can wait there.'

The man thought . . .

A nine-nine-nine call. Some sombre citizen heard a shot. Went to investigate, perhaps. Saw a badly wounded man. Saw another man in the water . . . a drowned man, perhaps. Cautiously. Gently. Because it is Saturday night, and drunks and hooligans claim Saturday night as their night. Nevertheless . . .

A little courage. A sense of civil duty. A peep over the bridge, and a glimpse of the towpath. Then a scurry to the nearest telephone kiosk.

A nine-nine-nine call.

Funny? Wouldn't you say? You—the world—wouldn't you say it was funny? That I'm already here. They don't even have to look. I'm already here . . . but they won't let me tell them!

10.30 p.m. . . .

They left the car in the park at the rear of Bordfield Headquarters, and entered by the rear door.

The station sergeant met them, and spoke to the uniformed superintendent.

'A triple-niner, sir. There's some trouble down on the canal bank. I've sent a squad car . . .'

'Cancel it,' snapped Lennox. 'We've sorted it out.'

'Oh! Yes, sir.' The sergeant looked puzzled, then said,

'Detective Constable Huggett . . .'

'Has he got Scarfe?' interrupted Lennox.

'Yes, sir. They're both in your office.'

'Good.'

'And there's a message for *you*, sir.'

'From?'

'Lessford. They've found some stolen property, in a disused warehouse.'

'Lovely grub.'

'It's on its way to Fingerprints . . . then Forensic Science.'

'And, it's all done by kindness.' Lennox turned to the uniformed superintendent, grinned, then added, 'Be a devil, Harry. Be in at the kill. That fancy uniform of yours might help . . . the Scarfes of this world go a bundle on baubles and insignias of rank.'

'Try to stop me,' chuckled the uniformed superintendent.

'Oh and, sergeant,' Lennox waved a hand to slow the uniformed sergeant on his way back to the innards of the police station. 'Phone my missus. Give her my apologies . . . and tell her she ain't gonna sell any kittens tonight, after all.'

Finney drove. Holmes sat, silent and scowling, in the front passenger seat.

Finney drove slowly. Pensively. Handling the car automatically, and with much of his mind elsewhere.

He muttered, 'We'll beat it.'

'What?' Holmes jerked out of his black study.

'Two to one,' said Finney. 'Page's word against ours. He slipped, and fell . . . that's our story.'

'Don't you ever give up?' asked Holmes, heavily.

'Not when I hold a winning hand.'

Holmes sighed, and said, 'Count me out.'

'Don't be a damn fool.'

'I've had enough of it.'

179

'Without your backing . . .'

'They'll get the truth, mate.' Anger, disgust and contempt bonded Holmes's words. 'Tomorrow morning, I go in there and tell the truth. No frills. No fancy excuses. You thumped Page, when it wasn't necessary. Because you enjoy thumping people. And I stood there, and watched. And, that makes us a couple of right bastards.'

'We had Scarfe,' snarled Finney. 'Dammit, doesn't that mean *anything*? We had . . .'

Holmes boiled over.

He rasped, 'Sod Scarfe! And, sod you! You're on the limb alone, Finney. Me? I'm thinking of myself—my wife and kid —from now on. I'll ride this thing out . . . but my way. I tell the truth. If necessary, I'll bring Page in, to verify every word I say. But, you're on your own, mate.'

'Of all the . . .'

'And, pull in to the kerb. I'll walk, from here. You want it straight, Finney? I don't like the company I'm in.'

10.40 p.m. . . .

Lennox was packing his pipe as he, and the uniformed superintendent, opened the door of his office and entered. D.C. Huggett drew himself into a position of semi-attention. From behind the desk—from Lennox's own chair—Scarfe smiled a cool welcome.

The uniformed superintendent closed the door.

Scarfe started, 'Good. I'm glad you've arrived, Lennox. I want you to . . .'

'*I* want you out of that chair,' snapped Lennox.

'Eh? Oh!—I'm sorry—I didn't realise . . .'

'You realised, all right,' said Lennox flatly. He turned to the D.C. 'The Official Caution, constable?'

'It's been administered, sir.'

'And?'

'His immediate reply was, "Get out of my way, you young fool".'

'Aye . . . it would be.'

Lennox waddled across the office and claimed his vacated chair. The uniformed superintendent stood, comfortably but ready, by the closed door. The detective constable waited, silent and eager to see how the big men did things. Scarfe moved from behind the desk, and made towards an empty chair, by the window.

'Don't sit down,' said Lennox.

'What?' Scarfe glared, and still bluffed.

'You'll only have to stand up, again.'

'Look—Lennox—I don't know what . . .'

'You know *exactly* "what". And, the rank's chief superintendent . . . assuming you can't bring yourself to say "sir".'

'Just who the devil . . .'

'We have the property,' snapped Lennox. 'It has your dabs all over it. We picked it up from where you left it, at the warehouse. We can prove your car was there—prove that it *went* there, prove that it *came away* from there. Before you're tucked up in a cell, we'll have those clothes and shoes you're wearing . . . then, we can prove *you* were there. That's the strength of the case, Scarfe. What you say, from here on in, is going to sound very silly . . . unless, of course, you care to name the thieves you bought the stuff from.'

It was a frontal attack. Every gun blazing . . . and it knocked all the fight from Scarfe. His face paled, he closed his eyes and, suddenly, he looked an old and broken man.

Lennox continued, 'There's also the little matter of your son-in-law. Detective Chief Inspector Finney. You conned him into being on the canal bank, tonight. Some tough lads were waiting for him . . . that's how I read things. Meanwhile, you decided to buy a kitten, and an alibi, at the same time. That's also how I read it . . . and, on a purely personal basis, I don't like being made the complete mug. Something went wrong. I dunno what . . . but that part will come. The tough lads weren't as tough as they thought they were. They didn't even *reach* Finney. We have two, and they'll talk . . . those kind always do.' Lennox paused, struck a match and, between puffs as he lighted his pipe, ended, 'That's about it, Scarfe. No bluff. The bare facts and, at a rough estimate, about a dozen charges you'll have dumped in your lap. There's a phone there . . . if you think you need a solicitor, use it.'

'No solicitor,' breathed Scarfe.

'It's your choice. Now, turn out your pockets . . . everything on the desk, here.' Lennox turned to the detective constable, and said, 'Check it, son. Then, search him, to make sure. After that, he's all yours. You made the arrest . . . he's your prisoner. Charge him. Handling stolen property . . . use that as a holding charge. We'll think of a few more things, later.'

'Yes, *sir*.' Huggett's eyes shone, at the prize he was being handed on a plate.

The uniformed superintendent's lips moved into a slow, approving smile. It was typical 'Lenny' tactics; recognise enthusiasm, then encourage it; don't grab the cherries . . . not when the cherries aren't needed, but might do somebody else a lot of good.

Lennox puffed at his pipe, and murmured, 'All that paperwork, son. Sooner you, than me.'

SUNDAY, JULY 15th . . .

2.45 a.m. . . .

Huggett ripped the last form, and two duplicates, from the typewriter, positioned them in their sequence in the three half-inch files on the desk in the C.I.D. Office, then pinched the top of his nose as a counter to his weariness.

'That it, son?' asked Lennox.

Huggett nodded.

'Worth it?' chuckled Lennox.

'For that pinch? Yes, sir—it's worth it . . . and, thanks.'

'You felt the collar, lad.' Lennox hauled himself from the chair he'd occupied for the last two hours. 'But, paper-work . . .' He waved a hand in disgust. 'Get used to it, son. My tea-leaves say you're going places and, the farther you go, the more bumpf you have to wade through.'

Huggett yawned and stretched, but looked contented.

Lennox said, 'Bed, son. Come in, this evening. Fix in the reports from Fingerprints and Forensic. Tie all the knots for a magistrate's hearing at ten o'clock, Monday morning . . . I'll have a word . . . we oppose bail. Come Monday, we'll think up a few more nooses for his neck. Now, go home and forget it.'

Huggett smiled, and said, 'Goodnight, sir.'

'Goodnight, son.'

Lennox lumbered from the C.I.D. Office and along the corridor. He opened the door of the Inner Charge Office, and said, 'I'm leaving now, sergeant. Have a quiet night.'

'Yes, sir. Goodn . . .'

'Sir!' The uniformed constable looked up from his task of logging the day's general police work. He turned his head, and spoke to the sergeant. 'There's the bloke in Number Three Interview Room, sergeant.'

'Oh, my Christ. Is he still there?'

'I haven't seen him leave.'

'What's that?' asked Lennox.

'Some nutter,' sighed the sergeant, then explained to Lennox the details of the visit of a stranger, and how that stranger had ended up in Number Three Interview Room . . . where, presumably, he still was.

'*He* must think it's important,' rumbled Lennox. 'I'll trot along and have a word with him.'

2.50 a.m. . . .

Lennox closed the door of Number Three Interview Room, and said, 'My name's Lennox. The bloke at the counter said you might still be here.'

'Are you a detective?' asked the man.

'Aye.' Lennox nodded.

'A senior detective?'

'Chief superintendent.'

'You'll do.'

'That's handsome of you, old son. What puzzles me is why you're still here. Three o'clock in the morning, thereabouts. A five-hour wait, so I'm told. Must be important.'

'Very important.'

'Ah, well.' Lennox lowered himself onto the spare chair. 'I suppose we'd better compare notes as to what is, and what isn't "important". You know my name. What about telling me yours?'

The man thought . . .

This stranger. This fat man, who claims to be a senior detective. Can I trust him? Can I really trust him? Because, if not —if there's a closing of ranks and a cover-up—it's all been wasted. It's all been for nothing, and I'm back at square one.

And yet, I have to trust somebody.

I have to trust a policeman.

Dear God, let there be at least one honest policeman around, and let this man be him.

3.10 a.m. . . .

Lennox said, 'What you've said, so far. You must have

184

gumption enough to know it's going to chase a few rabbits out of their holes. You've started an enquiry. Only you know where it might end. But—so far—you're in the clear. You're the injured party?' He paused, then said, 'It's what comes next that worries me.'

There was a silence. Lennox was angling for a reaction, but the man said nothing.

'All right,' sighed Lennox, 'we'll do things your way. 'Tape-recorder, and you can start from the beginning—then go on from there . . . agreed?'

'Agreed.'

'On the strict understanding. If you've bent the rules, whatever comes out isn't some sorta off-beat joke. You can stop, any time you like. If I ask any questions, that doesn't mean you have to answer 'em. And, if you feel you should have a solicitor in here with us, just ask . . . he'll be sent for.' Lennox stared across the table at the man, then said, 'That's it, son. My limitations, and your rights. Is everything clear?'

The man said, 'Very clear indeed . . . and, thank you.'

'So?' asked Lennox.

The man said, 'Set up your tape-recorder.'

The man thought . . .

Trustworthy? Possibly . . . but who knows? Not that it matters. Not at this stage.

But, not a written statement. That would be stupid. It would spoil everything. They use their own jargon, in written statements. They re-phrase things. They slip in a word here, leave out a word there, and it ends up their statement. Not yours. I've been caught once. But, not this time.

A tape-recording. They can't juggle with a tape-recording. My voice, telling my story. With every emphasis I want to be made. Then, the court will hear the truth. The unvarnished truth. The plain, lousy, stinking truth.

Certainly. A tape-recording.
My voice, telling my story.

4 a.m. . . .

'The gun?' asked Lennox, pointedly. 'The knife?'

The man said, 'Do you think I'd walk into a police station, tell this story . . . and bring the knife and gun with me?'

The man thought . . .

A lie. An implied lie. A very necessary lie, otherwise I don't succeed, nevertheless, a lie.

Will he take it? Will he accept it?

And, if he does take it, will it nullify everything else I've said? One lie . . . therefore it's all a pack of lies. That's the way the police mind works. One tiny lie, and destruction to everything else said.

Dear God, don't let that happen.

Let them accept this single lie, in isolation . . . but let them believe all the rest.

Otherwise . . .

5 a.m. . . .

The man sighed, then asked, 'Do you know what a "Joey" is?'

'Criminal slang,' said Lennox.

'Conboy called me a "Joey",' said the man. 'That's not my name . . . but that's what he called me.'

'Aye . . . I noticed.'

'You know what it means?' asked the man.

'I reckon,' growled Lennox.

The man said, 'In case you don't—in case you only half-know—let me tell you . . .'

The man thought . . .
The reason for all this. The reason for today. The reason for everything. The end of a twelve-year-old hate.
The only end.
The logical end . . . and the end I refuse you the right to deny me!

5.30 a.m. . . .

Lennox walked into the Inner Charge Office. Despite his bulk —despite his obesity—he looked crumpled, and older than his years. Tired, beyond mere physical weariness; tired, beyond the mere tiredness brought on by the lack of a night's sleep. Hopelessly tired. Helplessly tired. With bowed shoulders and arms which hung heavily by his sides.

The uniformed sergeant looked up from his desk, with a worried frown creasing his face.

He began, 'Sir. Are you . . .'

'We need some tea, sergeant.' Lennox's voice was little more than a hoarse whisper. 'We've had quite a session in Number Three Interview Room. We need . . .'

The single revolver shot echoed through the silent rooms and corridors of Bordfield Headquarters. It brought the sergeant, and the uniformed constable to their feet. Lennox closed his eyes, and moved his head slowly, in a single shake.

He opened his eyes, and said, 'Just one cup, sergeant.' Then, as the constable made for the door, he held out a hand, and said, 'Leave it, son. Get the coroner's officer. Then, get Deputy Chief Constable Sullivan. Ask him to come on duty . . . as a personal favour to me. To meet me in my office, as soon as possible.'

8.45 a.m. . . .

Lennox leaned across and pressed the 'stop' switch. The

recording of the revolver shot seemed to bounce from wall to wall of Lennox's office, as if it would never escape into silence.

Lennox raised his head and stared across at his colleague and friend, Richard Sullivan, Deputy Chief Constable.

'You let him do it?' There was near-disbelief in Sullivan's question.

Lennox nodded.

'For Christ's sake, why? *Why*, Lenny?'

'He hated coppers.' Lennox's voice was little more than a whispered groan. 'He mistrusted every damn copper in the world, Dick. Every one of 'em. It was his way of making sure there *couldn't* be a cover-up.'

'You knew he was going to do it?' Sullivan still couldn't quite believe it.

'I guessed.'

'And you left him? On the pretext of getting tea and biscuits?'

'It was as good an excuse as any.'

'For God's sake. The coroner'll skin you alive. Not searching him for the gun. Taking his word that he'd thrown it away. Then . . .'

'I'd a pretty good idea he hadn't thrown it away,' sighed Lennox.

'In that case . . .'

'Dick, don't be stupid,' pleaded Lennox. 'You, of all people. I was so bloody sure . . . that *you'd* understand.'

'All right,' said Sullivan, slowly. 'Try me. Let's say I'm slow on the uptake. Spell it out for me, Lenny. Whatever it is, I'm on your side . . . just reduce it to three-letter words. That's all.'

Lennox rubbed the stubble on his jowls, before he began. Then he spoke slowly. With compassion. With a depth of understanding which sat awkwardly on his gross frame.

He said, 'Like I say, he hated coppers. Twelve years ago, he committed an offence. A crime. Rape. Technically, it was rape . . . nobody's disputing that. *Factually*, though . . . factually, *she* raped *him*. We both know it happens. The easiest accusation in the world to make . . . the hardest to disprove. Then, up comes Finney. He was motor patrol, at that time. Finney and the Scarfe girl . . . they knew each other. Finney. Ambitious, even in those days. He knew old man Scarfe was going places . . . already had the ear of influential people. So-o, he cooked the evidence. *Really* cooked the evidence. He cooked it well enough to pin an eighteen-year lagging to the tail of a very technical offence.

'Y'get it Dick?' Lennox's voice was sad. 'A first brush with the police, and that's what happens. Then, twelve years in the company of men who hate coppers. Men who swear they were "fixed" . . . and, they all do. Maybe he didn't believe all of it. But, he believed some. Enough. That's why the tape-recording. He was after Finney, from the second he walked out of those gates . . . but, he wanted to be sure. No written statements. No official complaints, with forms attached. He wanted to tell the world, in his own words. He was sure—he was damn *sure*—we'd do a cover-up job, if he tried it any other way. His words. His voice. That way, we couldn't sweep it under the carpet.'

'And, the gun?' asked Sullivan, gently. 'The knife?'

Lennox linked his fingers across his pot-belly, and said, 'The knife was in case he couldn't get a gun. That easy. That obvious. But, he got his hands on a gun . . . and that's what he wanted. A "frightener" . . . that's all. He didn't intend to kill anybody. He'd no intention of *shooting* anybody.'

Lennox sighed, and shook his head, as he continued, 'The damndest thing. He knew—maybe instinctively—something I proved, on the bowling green. Something Finney himself proved. That, once a man's told a story, he'll repeat that story without much effort. Without much pushing. Page . . . Finney had to knock Page about, before he coughed. But *I* didn't.

Page repeated the info, without me even asking for it. He'd done it once . . . after that, it was easy. The same with Finney's wife. Wave a gun at her. Force her to tell the truth—scare her into it . . . she'll repeat the truth, every time she's asked, from then on. Like uncorking a bottle. From then on, you just pour out the wine.

'He wanted to do the same with Finney, but things went a little wrong. That cock-up's being seen to. The Leeds boys are working on it. It's linked in with Conboy, somewhere . . . we'll find out where, eventually. But, he didn't intend to *kill* Finney. I'll stake my life on it. Just scare a confession out of him. Like with Finney's wife.'

'And Chambers?' Sullivan asked the question, even though he thought he knew the answer.

'Oh, come on, Dick,' protested Lennox. 'That was a test . . . nothing more, nothing less. He knew about his wife's affair with Tim Chambers. What he didn't know was whether Chambers was serious. He threatened to kill him, if Chambers didn't stop seeing his wife. Chambers told him to go to hell . . . and that's all he needed. He was convinced.'

'And then,' said Sullivan, grimly, 'he strolls into the biggest nick in the district, and blows his brains out . . . bloody wonderful!'

'Damn it, Dick. It was what it was all *about*. Look . . .' Lennox leaned forward slightly, unlinked his fingers and used his hands to emphasise his words. 'Two reasons. To him, two very *good* reasons. If you had those reasons you, too, might have done it.

'First of all, this business of being a "Joey". Get it. Grab it. And try to understand what it means. Those first few months in prison. He was hammered. He was crippled . . . because, he was a "child rapist". Always the genitals. Every time— damn near every day—boots, knives, knees . . . and always in the privates. In and out of hospital. Now, look—forget about castration . . . it was a damn sight more than that. He was neutered. Completely! Castrate a man, and he's still capable of an erection. He can't father kids . . . but that's the only thing he *can't* do. But hammer a man hard enough—long enough—injure a man enough times, and something much more drastic happens. He becomes completely sexless. The only thing left for him, in that line, is being the passive partner in a homosexual relationship . . . and his genes, plus his natural disgust at the idea, wouldn't let him do that. That's what being a "Joey" means. Being a *nothing*. Good God, man . . . think of it. The prime of his life. A man who was once normal —virile . . . and now nothing!

'That's *really* why he hated Finney. And that's why he shot himself.

'In a police station? Where else? After he'd taped his story? *What* else? That tape was his suicide note . . . the equivalent. He knew there'd be a coroner's inquest. He knew the whole of that tape would *have* to be listened to, by a coroner's court. Which—as far as he was concerned—meant that there couldn't be a cover-up. It was his way. As he thought, the only certain way. To destroy Finney and his wife. To make sure they *had* to be destroyed. And, at the same time, to check that his own wife was going to be taken care of.'

'To commit suicide?' Sullivan shook his head in sad disgust.

'He didn't trust us, Dick . . . that's the root cause.' Lennox rubbed the back of his neck, and ended, 'All he had to do was complain. Make an official complaint. Finney's on rocky ground, already. His wife . . . he could have divorced her. So many other ways. But he didn't trust any of 'em. He went out with a bullet . . . because he'd once come across a corrupt copper. Jesus! What a waste.'

Sullivan scowled his concern at the carpet, then murmured, 'The coroner will give you hell, Lenny. That gun . . . he'll give you hell.'

'I'll take it,' said Lennox, grimly. 'But, believe me, I'll pass it on, with interest, to Finney. He's finished. Him, or me. There's no room for us both in the same force.'